Candi & Mandy's Cozies

A COLLECTION OF SHORT STORIES

JOAN BRUCE

ISBN: 978-1-970730-91-3

Cover design by Candice Cooper

Published by

Fideli Publishing, Inc.
119 W. Morgan St.
Martinsville, IN 46151
www.FideliPublishing.com

Dedication

To my very smart and
beautiful granddaughters:
Sarah, Tiffany, Abby & Nadia

Introduction

What's a guy in his late Seventies doing writing short stories about a pair of forty something women?

Good question. And, before your mind wanders too far afield, let me explain how Candi DeCarlo and Mandy Malone became my two favorite protagonists.

It began in 2007. The Speed City Chapter of Sisters in Crime had just formed. They were set to publish their first anthology, "*Racing Can Be Murder*," featuring 19 stories about the annual Indy 500 race.

My submission. "Murder in the Snake Pit," focused on Charley O'Brien. He was a local all-night radio talk show host who began reminiscing about the track's infamous snake pit and a murder that occurred there in 1981.

After finishing my first draft, I realized my story had no female callers. Enter Candi and Mandy. They just left a local bar and had flipped on their car radio. Turns out they witnessed the murder and gave Charley valuable information to help identify the murderer. The second draft was much better. And, I had fallen in love with Candi and Mandy.

Two years later, Speed City published its second anthology, *Bedlam at the Brickyard*, featuring stories about the Brickyard 400 NASCAR race. My story, "I Love You, Jeff Gordon," told how a Tony Stewart fan harassed Candi before the race. When the guy was later found dead after the race, Candi became the prime suspect. The story follows Candi as she looks for the real killer. Turns out it was the dead guy's girlfriend, who looked like Candi and wore an identical Jeff Gordon T-shirt.

The next story in this anthology is entitled "Chasin' Cooter." It is an unpublished NASCAR story featuring a former car mechanic who killed his former sister-in-law in Bartonsville, Indiana, the mythical town where Candi and Mandy live.

Stories four and five, "Rescuing My Ex," and "Mom's Prince Charming," also were unpublished. They were written primarily to "test" Candi's relationship with her ex-husband, Bobby DeCarlo and her mother, Wanda Mae Thompson.

Bobby is accused of murdering a motorcycle gang member during a bar fight. Candi comes to his rescue and discovers that Bobby is innocent. The murderer was a fellow gang member.

This story provided me with some background for my second, soon-to-be published novel, *"Nail Biter: The Mystery of the Clobbered Coach,"* where Bobby becomes the town's interim high school football coach.

Wanda Mae didn't appear in Candi's first novel, *"Hangnails: The Mystery of the Butchered Banker,"* but she'll be in future novels, thanks to the "relationship" developed with her daughter in this story.

"No Love in the Tub" has Candi and Mandy employing a psychic, Madame Filina, to learn who murdered their high school friend, Patsy Slocum, in her hot tub.

"That Ugly Painting," follows Candi as she tracks down who stole the abstract painting she bought at a local estate sale. The painting once belonged to a well-known Indianapolis art collector.

Editors of anthologies often focus on annual holidays like Halloween and Christmas. The remaining five stories reflect that interest.

Of the three Halloween stories, "Candy Bars" was unpublished. In it, I wanted to show how civic-minded Candi and Mandy were in donating candy and their time to a school Halloween party. The story also shows how Candi came to Mandy's defense when the parents of a boy who had an allergic reaction to a candy bar wanted to sue her.

"Murder in the Corn Maze," published in 2009, was actually my second published short story. Candi is not the protagonist. Instead, it's Martha Rae Folger of the town's radio station. I don't remember why this happened other than Candi wouldn't have had any direct connection to a corn maze. Martha Rae did because her employee, Carolyn Tinsdale, the station's news and farm editor, also owned a farm. This story also introduced Johnny Edwards, who later became Candi's sidekick in solving murders.

"Harvey's House of Horrors" is another Speed City anthology. Candi and Mandy decide to relive a youthful memory by visiting the local haunted house only to find that the son of the original owner has been murdered.

The final two stories, "Away in the Manger" and "The Mysterious Mincemeat Murder" are about Christmas. The unpublished manger story features Emma Lou Pettijohn, an elderly widow who steals the baby Jesus from a local church manger because she's worried the baby isn't wearing any warm clothes.

Emma Lou returns in the final story where Candi invites her and Mandy to help at a Christmas Eve dinner at the local assisted-living facility. An elderly man is poisoned after eating one of Emma Lou's mincemeat tarts. Candi interviews the man's female dinner companions to find the murderer.

What is my favorite short story? Definitely "Away in the Manger." It shows Candi's Christmas spirit in buying two baby Jesus replacement dolls and in befriending a new friend, Emma Lou Pettijohn.

P.S. If you enjoyed any of these stories, you may want to buy Candi's first full-length novel, *"Hangnails: The Mystery of the Butchered Banker"* wherever books are sold on the internet.

Joan Bruce
November 2025

Table of Contents

Candi & Mandy's Cozies

Murder in the Snake Pit

"And then there was that time in '81 when this guy was murdered in the snake pit."

Phil from Greenwood had been droning on for ten minutes about his memories of the Indy 500 when he dropped that bomb. Unfortunately, I was overdue for a commercial break. Believe it or not, we do sell airtime on my all-night radio talk show.

"Hang on, Phil. I've got to sell some stuff. But when we come back, I want to hear more."

My producer, Zack Berman, punched up the commercials from our second-floor control room, while I waited impatiently in the studio next door. It's no bigger than a phone booth and is used for news breaks during the day. Management doesn't want us using the main studio on the first floor that faces onto Monument Circle. They're afraid too many drunks will rap on the window at night if we do our show from there. I've worked in bigger studios in my career, but I have to say the computer equipment at WZMN-AM, News Talk Radio 790, is state-of-the-art.

Right now, though, none of that mattered. I was more interested in finding out if I'd heard Phil correctly. A murder in the snake pit? The pit used to have an "anything goes" reputation in its heyday, but murder? That seemed a little far-fetched. Maybe Phil was just spinning an urban yarn.

"Okay, folks, we're back," I said when the last commercial ended. "It's twenty after the hour. I'm Charley O'Brien. Before the break, Phil from Greenwood was telling us about a murder in the snake pit back in '81. Who was murdered?"

"Freddie Olds."

"Did you know him?"

"Nope."

"Anything more you want to say?"

"Don't know much more, Charley. Freddie's story didn't surface until a few days after the race. His family must have reported him missing. Anyway, the cops learned he'd been in the snake pit with some friends on race day, but nobody saw him leave. It was like he disappeared into thin air. The local TV stations had a field day. They showed nightly video clips of Boy Scout troops helping the cops look for Freddie in every nook and cranny. When the cops didn't find him after a week, the media lost interest and that was that."

"Sounds more like Freddie just disappeared."

"But word on the street has always been that he was murdered. The cops couldn't prove it, though. No body and no crime scene to speak of after a party like that. A sheriff's deputy I once knew told me the cops couldn't find any credible eyewitnesses. Nobody saw anything."

"Thanks for telling us that story, Phil."

Eight months ago, I moved back to Indy to start this all-night talk show after being away nearly thirty years. I grew up in the shadow of the Indianapolis Motor Speedway, and talk of a murder in the snake pit made me real curious. I wondered if any other listeners knew about Freddie Olds. I asked them and didn't have to wait long for an answer. Wayne McLean's name popped up on my computer.

"What's on your mind this morning, Wayne?"

"I knew Freddie Olds."

"You did? Tell us about him. Were you buddies?"

"Sort of. He used to date my sister, Margie. He treated her pretty good. For Valentine's Day, he even bought her some earrings that looked like fishing lures."

"The message on my computer screen says you're from the Westside. You probably went to the race every year, right?"

"Yeah, we were all there. Me and my pals. Knockin' back a few out of the bed of my pal's pickup. Freddie and his pals were sittin' on a blue-striped couch next to us, eyeing the babies and having a few beers themselves."

"How'd that couch end up in the pit?"

"Bobby Matthews had it in his big red van. He was one of Freddie's pals."

"So when did Freddie disappear?"

"I don't know."

"What do you mean?"

"Didn't see the end of the race. I passed out with fifty laps to go. Must have been the heat and the cold beer. You gotta watch that when you have pale skin. My pals picked me up and tossed me in the back of their pickup. Didn't come to for three or four hours."

"Hmmm. Did any of your friends see what happened to Freddie?"

"Nope. They were too busy talking to everybody who walked by and asked about me. 'Is he dead?' folks would say. 'He looks dead.'" Pretty soon my pals started telling everyone that I died from heat stroke. They were even gonna charge folks a quarter for a peek. How funny is that?"

"Pretty funny. Too bad about the heat stroke. I was hoping you'd help us solve the Freddie Olds mystery."

It was 1:35 a.m. Time for another two-minute commercial break. The Freddie Olds story was beginning to pique my interest. Even though Wayne hadn't been much help, at least he'd confirmed that Freddie was at the track in '81 with some guy named Bobby Matthews. That was a start, I guess.

When we went live again, Raymond from Indianapolis was holding on Line One.

"How can I help you this morning?"

"I just heard you talking to that guy, Wayne. Heard him telling you about Freddie Olds and all, so I thought I'd call, too."

"Great. What can you add to the story?"

"He was an okay dude. Freddie, that is. We used to work together. We were welders. Freddie was a guy who'd give you the T-shirt off his back. But he couldn't hold his liquor. When he got drunk, he'd do crazy things.

"He once told me how he got arrested for drag racing down Madison Avenue. Turns out the other car was an unmarked police cruiser. Stuff like that."

"Were you with him at the track in '81?"

"Naw, we never hung out much. I was married back then, and didn't drink neither. That day, I drove my old lady to a family reunion. Besides, I've never really liked Indy cars. I prefer NASCAR."

"What about Freddie's friends, Bobby Matthews" Know anything about him?"

"Never met the guy, but Freddie once told me that Bobby was a bad-ass dude. Apparently did time at Pendleton. Beat up a bartender real bad."

"Did Freddie disappear or was he murdered?"

"If I was a bettin' man, I'd say he was murdered."

Another vote for murder. This story definitely was getting better. It was beginning to sound like Freddie got crossways with somebody. All I needed now was to hear from someone who was there that day and saw what happened. Maybe this mystery might get solved after all.

"Hiiiiiiiiii, Charleeeeee."

"Is this Candi from Indianapolis?"

Zach had typed her name across my computer screen.

"Yeah," she breathed heavily into the phone.

"Whoa, Candi. Turn down your radio. I'm getting too much feedback."

As Candi dropped her phone to fix the radio, I thought I heard someone in the background.

"Hi, Charley, it's me, Mandy. Did anyone ever tell you that you have a sexy voice? And I bet you are a real hunk, too."

I hated to shatter Mandy's fantasy, so I took the more chivalrous path and kept quiet, hoping Candi would come back on the line soon.

"I'm back, Charley."

"What's happening with you two lovely ladies this morning?"

"You're such a sweet talker, Charley. No wonder Mandy's sitting here cooling her forehead with a beer bottle. We just left Pete's Hideaway Lounge on Lynhurst and flipped on the car radio. Heard you talking about poor Freddie Olds, so we decided to call."

"Did you know Freddie?"

"Hell yes. Every girl on the Westside knew Freddie. He was a little bitty guy, but nobody seemed to notice, if you get my drift. And he was one damn fine kisser. He used to get me all fired up. What about you, Mandy?"

Great. Turns out Freddie was some kind of a love machine. I really wasn't interested in knowing that. I just wanted to find out if anybody saw him get murdered.

"Ladies, can I get you to focus on other parts of Freddie's personality?"

"Other parts. That's funny. Mandy, did you hear what Charley said? About Freddie's other parts."

I was beginning to think Candi and Mandy were a lost cause when Candi piped up.

"We were there that day. We saw what happened to Freddie."

As Candi dropped that revelation, I heard Zach rap on the large picture window that separates the control room from my studio. I hadn't been watching the clock. Time for the Fox News feed at the top of the hour. Damn. I was afraid I'd lose Candi and Mandy if I put them on hold. Then I got an idea.

"Does Mandy own a cell phone?"

"Sure," Candi replied. "Why?"

"'Cause I want to do a three-way."

"Charleeeee."

"Nothing like that. Have her call in like you did. Zach will patch her into our conversation so we can all talk at once. How's that?"

"Mandy, find your cell and call Charley."

Good. That should keep them busy during the ninety second news break and the two minutes of commercials. I ran next door and told Zach to tape Candi and Mandy. I had a hunch that once they got talking, they might say something worthwhile about Freddie. I also took Maria Rodriguez's business card from my wallet and handed it to Zach. "Call and have her listen to the show." Maria is a homicide detective with the Indianapolis Metropolitan Police Department and an occasional dining companion.

I rushed back to my studio. In the interim, Mandy had found her phone, dialed our number and was hooked up with Candi and me.

"Okay, folks, we're back," I said. "Let's pick up where we left off. Ladies, tell me more about Freddie Olds being at the track in '81."

"He was pretty drunk," Mandy began. "He started passing out free beer to any girl who'd show him her assets."

"Where were you two?"

"Standing next to him, drinking a few free beers," Candi said. "Then Bobby Matthews gets mad. Says Freddie is giving away too much beer and there won't be enough left for them."

"What happened next?"

"Freddie started mouthing back. Says he paid for part of the beer keg and he wants to look at some more assets."

"Then what?"

"Bobby jumps up off the couch and pushes Freddie to the ground. Then Freddie gets up and tries to wrestle with Bobby. They grab and clutch each other and fall backwards over the beer keg and the tube of ice it's sitting in."

"Yeah, then the whatchamacallit falls off the keg and beer starts spilling all over the ground."

"The whatchamacallit?"

"What's the name of that thing, Mandy?"

"You mean the doohickey?"

"Yeah, maybe that's what it's called."

"Ladies, can one of you please describe the whatchamacal-lit or doohickey?"

"It's that hard metal thing on top of the beer keg."

"The beer tap?"

"That's it."

"So, the beer tap somehow comes loose."

"Yeah, beer is spilling all over the place," Mandy said. "Bobby picks up the doohickey and whacks Freddie over the head with it. Freddie falls down. Then Bobby walks over and fixes the keg like nothing happened."

"Yeah, everybody is pointing and laughing at poor Freddie," Candi said. "Bobby pours a beer on his head, but Freddie doesn't move. Bobby reaches down and pokes Freddie, but then Bobby jumps up and whispers something to his pals. Next thing you know, they hoist the couch in the van. Then they scoop up Freddie and throw him on top of the couch and take off."

"Did anybody do anything?"

"Wayne McLean's friends wandered over and picked up the beer keg and bucket of ice and threw it in their truck," Mandy said.

"What did you two do?"

"I can't remember exactly. Mandy, didn't we walk over and have a beer with Wayne's friends?"

"Yeah, and then we headed for the exit. The race was nearly over and we wanted to beat the crowd."

"Why didn't you call the police and tell them what happened to Freddie?"

"That he got whacked on the head by one of his pals?"

"You didn't think it was more serious than that?"

"What are you trying to say, Charley?" Candi said defensively. "That we aren't good citizens or whatever?"

"Nothing like that. I just thought that when you heard later how Freddie was reported missing, you might have called the cops and told them what you knew."

"We never listen to the news, Charley," Mandy said. "It's too depressing. Besides, why would we want to cross Bobby? He's a bad ass. We once heard how he reached across a bar one night and cracked open a bartender's skull with a beer bottle 'cause the guy wouldn't serve him last call."

I looked up at the clock. It was 2:18 a.m. I'd been on the phone with Candi and Mandy for almost a half-hour. I was mentally drained. And with all that effort, I still didn't know if Freddie Olds had been murdered or if he simply had disappeared with a big lump on his head.

I thanked Candi and Mandy for their time, reminded Mandy that it was against station policy to date my listeners and asked them to stay on the line so Zach could get their last names and home numbers. I figured that if anything came of our conversation, Maria would want to talk to them.

As I waited for the latest commercials to end, I rubbed my eyes before peering down at my computer. Was I reading Zach's message correctly? Bobby Matthews was holding on Line One.

"What's going on this morning, Bobby?" I said nonchalantly.

"You that Charley guy? Just got home from work. Wayne says he done called you a ways back. Says you a right nice feller. I should call you and tell you about Freddie Olds myself."

"That's right. Was he a friend of yours?"

"You talkin' of Wayne?"

"Sure," I replied. I really didn't care how well Bobby knew Wayne McLean. I just wanted him to stay on the line and talk to me. "How long have you known him?"

"Probably thirty years. I used to date his sister, Margie, for a time. Me and Wayne are roomies now on account of how his old lady done throwed him out last month and I had an empty couch.

That was more than I really wanted to know. I took a deep breath and pressed on.

"Interesting, Bobby, but let me ask you. Were you at the track in '81? That's the year Bobby Unser won his third Indy 500 race."

"I remember that race. Them Unser boys were damn fine racers."

"Let me ask you another question. What kind of vehicle did you drive back then?"

"Big red van. Had large curly yellow waves on each side. Sure did. Why you askin'?"

"Just wondering. I had a yellow Corvair myself. Remember them? The engine was in the rear. A really dorky-looking car, but it was all I could afford. I was a DJ back then. I didn't make much money. But my Corvair got decent gas mileage. Wish I had her today with gas prices as high as they are."

Damn. I shouldn't have spent so much time trying to ease Bobby into a conversation about Freddie Olds. Now I'll probably never find out what he knew about Freddie's disappearance.

We went to another commercial break and took a few other calls before I noticed Bobby's name on my computer screen again.

"Is that you, Bobby? What happened?"

"I had to shake the worm and gets a beer. Workin' sure makes a feller thirsty."

"Let's pick up where we left off. You were telling us about your big red van. It must have been a real chick magnet. Bet you had a mattress in the back in case you got lucky with the ladies.

"Huh, I had a couch. Used it for love engagements, and then I'd pull it out at the drive-in."

"By the way, what color was it?"

"I had blue stripes."

"Wow, my neighbor's looking for a couch with blue stripes. Still got it?"

"Been thirty years, man. It's long gone."

"What did you do with it?"

"Why you askin'?"

"Just trying to make late-night conversation."

"Dumped it on my daddy's farm."

"Now, did I ask if you knew Freddie Olds?"

"You sure ask lots of questions. Me, Freddie and my pal, Pete Gibson, were tight."

"Somebody told me that you and Freddie were at the track in '81 and Freddie disappeared before the race was over."

"It were that shit, Wayne, weren't it? That big mouth. Mouths off when he's drunk. Can I say 'shit' on the radio?"

"Sorry, Bobby, you can't. The FCC is very anal when it comes to words like that. They love to fine us, but we have a 10-second taped delay system, so my producer caught it and bleeped you."

"You're taping me? I don't like that. I'm hanging up."

"No, no, Bobby. Don't do that. Calm down. We throw the tape away after every show."

I didn't hear anything on the other end of the line, but it didn't sound like Bobby had hung up. What's he doing now?

"Friggin' phone fell on the floor. What was we talkin' about? Right, that shit, Wayne."

"Wayne told me that he passed out during the race. His buddies threw him in the back of their pickup. Everybody thought he was dead. But Wayne said it was just heat stroke. Right, like I believe that."

"I remember now. That silly little shit. Can't hold his liquor."

"What's that noise in the background?"

"A siren, dude."

Maria to the rescue? I decided to go ahead and ask the sixty-four thousand dollar question.

"Why did you whack Freddie over the head with a beer tap?"

"What?"

"And why did you leave the beer keg behind?"

"Man, you knows too much. I'm gonna kill that Wayne."

Bobby slammed down the phone. I didn't care. The sirens sounded even closer than before. I hoped Maria and her colleagues arrested him. I'd call her when my show ended at five and find out for sure. And I can already imagine our conversation.

"Why do you keep trying to solve every murder that happens in Indianapolis?" she'd ask. "I thought we'd straightened that out after the last murder. Remember? You agreed. I'm the crime fighter; you're the all-night talk show host."

"Yeah, right," I'd reply. "Let's go grab some breakfast."

Originally published in the
Racing Can Be Murder Anthology, *Blue River Press, 2007.*

I Love You, Jeff Gordon

"Jeff Gordon!" the voice bellowed so loudly it practically shook the ground under my feet.

I turned to see who'd swallowed the megaphone and spotted this little guy in a neon orange Tony Stewart T-shirt that barely stretched across his gut. His blue jean shorts hung just above his knees. And he had a death grip on his can of beer. Two dorks in matching outfits stood behind Mr. Pumpkin Man.

"What'd you say?"

"I said I hate Jeff Gordon," the guy barked louder than before.

Several racing fans had formed a wide circle around us. No doubt they were hoping pudgy and I would start wrestling with each other in front of the Indianapolis Motor Speedway.

"What's your problem, mister?" I asked.

"You deaf? I hate Jeff Gordon," he replied before taking a healthy swig of his beer and wiping his mouth off with the back of his arm. "Gordon's a wuss, and anybody who loves him is a wuss, too."

It was all I could do to keep from kicking the guy where it would hurt, but I didn't. I was wearing flip flops. Instead, I just glared at him and said, "Get a life, fatso."

As I turned back to my friend Mandy Malone, she grabbed me by the arm.

"Look out, Candi," she yelled.

Without looking up, I did a quick two-step as Mr. Roly-Poly tripped over his shoelaces and fell flat on his face beside me.

"Now, look at what you've done," Fatso said as he tried picking himself up. "You've made me spill my beer. You owe me a drink."

"In your dreams, buster."

I grabbed Mandy's arm and steered her toward the gate that would take us to our seats in the grandstands.

"What was Fatso's problem?" I asked her as we sat down in our seats.

"I think it was your T-shirt."

"What's wrong with it?"

"Oh, I don't know," Mandy said as she squirted suntan lotion on her arms. "Maybe it's Jeff Gordon's picture on the front or the 'I Love You, Jeff Gordon' lettering on the back."

"Isn't it great?" I said, pulling my shirt out in front of me so I could get a better look at Jeff's gorgeous face. "I won it last week on WYMN. Besides these seats, I also got two pit passes to meet Jeff afterward. Just for telling Martha Rae Folger's listeners in 30 seconds or less why I love Jeff Gordon."

"Why didn't you bring Bobby?" Mandy asked. "Isn't he a big NASCAR fan?"

"Bobby's a huge fan, but he's mad at me because I won and he didn't. Bobby choked up on air and nothing came out."

"Sounds like your marriage," Mandy said. "Oops, I didn't mean to say that. It just popped out."

"Don't worry, I replied. "Bobby's biggest problem was forgetting to come home at night. He's history now, but you're gonna be hooked on NASCAR before this race is over."

"Don't count on it."

The Brickyard 400 was terrific. After a four-car pileup on the 14th lap, the race settled down to an exciting duel between Jeff Gordon and Tony Stewart. But on the final lap, Jeff's car was bumped from behind and Jimmie Johnson roared past him.

"Okay," Mandy said as she stood up in her seat. "I admit the race wasn't too bad after all. Ready to go?"

"We're not going anywhere," I quickly reminded her. "Don't you remember, I won pit passes to meet Jeff in person."

"Do we have to?" Mandy whined.

"Absolutely," I replied. "Jeff is going to pick the grand prize winner."

"And what's the winner get? A giant hug from your hero?"

"Don't I wish! No, it's an authentic red leather team jacket."

"Whoopee."

Mandy and I were about halfway to Jeff's garage in Gasoline Alley when I spotted a restroom just head of us.

"I need to go potty," I said turning to Mandy. "Want to come?"

"No, I'll stay here and watch everyone else leave," she said.

I hurried into the restroom and quickly found an empty stall. As I sat there checking out the tiles at my feet, the woman in the next stall appeared to want to play a game of footsies. Part of her orange running shoe was sticking under the partition over on my side.

I coughed a few times, hoping she'd take the hint, but her shoe didn't move. I stood up, flushed the toilet, and quickly left the stall. I fully intended to wash my hands and quickly leave, but a tiny voice inside my head suddenly told me that I should check on the woman in the next stall. What if she wasn't one of those funny gals after all, and she was sick and had passed out on the floor? I walked over to her stall and tapped on the door.

"Is everything OK in there?" I asked politely.

No answer. I rapped a little harder. This time, the door slowly swung open. And sitting on the floor was Fatso in his neon orange T-shirt. A hot dog was sticking out of his mouth.

"What are you doing in here?" I shouted.

He didn't answer, so I quickly ran out of the restroom to find some help.

"What's the matter?" Mandy asked as I ran toward her. "You look like you've seen a ghost."

"Worse," I said, trying to catch my breath. "It's Fatso, He's lying dead inside."

"What?" Mandy exclaimed. "Why would he be in there?"

"Beats me, but he is. And it looks like he choked on a hot dog."

"Well, we can't just leave him there," Mandy said, reaching into her purse and pulling out her cell phone. "Women need to use that restroom. Let's call 9-1-1."

About 10 minutes later, a tall, good-looking guy walked up to us. The two dorks were in tow.

"I'm Detective Dan Parker of the Speedway Police Department," he said, flashing his badge. "What's the problem?"

"In there," I said, pointing to the restroom.

The detective ran into the restroom with the dorks right behind him. They emerged a minute later.

"We need to talk, miss," Detective Parker said as he approached. "These two men just told me you confronted their friend earlier today and threatened him."

"So...."

"That's him inside the restroom," the detective said. "These men have identified him. They haven't seen him since he went for some food more than an hour ago. They were worried that something happened to him. That's why they stopped me a while ago and asked if I could help them find their friend."

"And you did," I said. "Good police work on your part, detective."

Detective Parker wasn't amused. He just glared at me.

"You've got some serious questions to answer about all of this," he said firmly. "But first I need to call for some help. Then I'm taking you to the police station."

A few minutes later, Detective Parker stuck Mandy and me in the backseat of a big black police cruiser. The air inside suddenly felt like we were stuck inside a meat locker. Mandy didn't say a word and refused to look at me.

When we arrived at the police station, Detective Parker put me and Mandy in separate interrogation rooms. I got stuck talking to a middle-aged detective with a cheap toupee.

"So, Ms. DeCarlo," Detective Hairpiece began, "what exactly did you say to Leonard Walton?"

"Who?"

"The deceased. I understand you threatened him before the race began."

"I just called him Fatso. That's not a threat. It's a fact of life."

"Maybe so, but what were the two of you doing inside that restroom?" the detective asked as he glanced across the table at me.

"Not what you're thinking," I said, glaring at him. "I needed to go, and he was already in there. End of story."

As Detective Hairpiece stared at me, a uniformed officer wandered into the room and whispered something in the detective's ear. The cop must have brushed up against his toupee because it suddenly looked slightly off center. The two of them left and I was left to wonder what would happen next.

About 15 minutes later, the detective returned. He told me Mandy had vouched for my whereabouts during the Brickyard 400 and had mentioned how I'd simply slipped into the restroom on our way to Jeff Gordon's garage.

Didn't I say that a half hour ago?

"I'm going to drive you back to your vehicle now, Ms. DeCarlo," the detective said. "We still need to do an autopsy on Mr. Walton. But you're still a 'person of interest' in my book."

Tips & Toes, where I work as a manicurist, is closed on Mondays so I usually spend the morning doing my laundry at Sun & Suds, Bartonsville's combination laundromat and tanning parlor. I was sitting there on a red plastic chair, reading an old gossip magazine, when my cell phone rang.

"Is that you, Candi?" Martha Rae Folger asked.

"What's up?"

"I just read a news story about an unidentified woman finding a guy dead inside a woman's restroom at the track yesterday," she said. It reminded me of you and the Jeff Gordon contest. How'd you make out?"

"I won the booby prize," I replied. "I'm the one who found that guy."

"You're the one who found Lenny Walton? Is he still as chunky as ever?"

"You know him?"

"If he's the same one I knew while growing up on the eastside of Indy. I used to babysit a fat little kid by that name. I suppose it could be him."

"Did the story say anything else?" I asked.

"Only that the cops questioned the woman and later released her," Martha Rae said. "But a Detective Harrington is quoted as saying she remains 'a person of interest." Candi, do the cops really think you killed Lenny?"

"That detective does, but I didn't do it."

"I believe you, sweetie. Is there anything I can do to help?"

"Yeah, give me Lenny's old address. Maybe one of his relatives still lives there, and they'll tell me how he ended up in the restroom with a hot dog stuck in his mouth."

After Martha Rae had given me Lenny's address, I started making plans for my trip to Indianapolis. A bunch of questions flooded my brain.

Like, if the cops still planned to do an autopsy on Lenny, maybe they didn't think the hot dog was to blame for his death. Could it have been something else? Did the cops think that somebody actually murdered him and used the hot dog to help cover up the crime? And why was Lenny in that restroom in the first place? He didn't seem like the drag queen type.

I left Sun & Suds with my laundry basket tucked under my arm and jumped into my Ford F-150. It took me nearly an hour before I pulled up in front of a dilapidated two-story white house on East Washington Street in Indianapolis.

I walked up on the creaky porch and knocked on the front door. A moment later, a tiny, white-haired woman in a faded blue housecoat peered around the heavy brown door and snapped, "What do you want?"

So that's where Lenny got his winning personality?

I wasn't about to let this old lady slam the door in my face, so I quickly told her about meeting Lenny at the track and how sweet he seemed. I know I lied. Sue me. I finished by asking her if Lenny had any friends or enemies.

"He used to hang around with the Shaw twins, Steve and Cleave," she replied. "And then there's his ex-girlfriend, Molly Pollock. She looks a little like you, only younger. Lenny lived with her until she wised up and threw his sorry butt out a couple months back. He begged me to let him live here. I'm sure Lenny had some enemies, but I don't know who they are."

"Where can I find Molly Pollock?" I asked.

"Hold on," the woman said. "I've got her address and phone number written down somewhere. I'll just be a minute."

After Granny stepped away from the doorway, I glanced at my Betty Boop watch. Not quite 2 o'clock. Once I had Molly's number, I'd call and talk to her for a few minutes before heading home. With any luck, I could still enjoy a 30-minute bake at Sun & Suds before dinner.

The old woman returned a minute later with Molly's information. I mentioned Lenny's winning personality again.

"Yeah, right," she replied with a look of disbelief. "My grandson was about as sweet as a rattlesnake."

Back in my truck, I quickly dialed Molly's number. No answer. Granny also had given me directions to Molly's apartment in Beech Grove, so I drove over there and left a note in her mailbox. I'd call her later. I had just turned south onto State Road 37 for my ride home when my cell went off.

"Where are you?" Mandy asked.

"On my way home from Indy," I replied. "What's up?"

"I just had a call from Mary Donovan at the Bartonsville Police Department. She didn't have your cell number. The Speedway cops are looking for you. They found some witnesses earlier today, and they want to do a police lineup. You'll need to bring your Jeff Gordon T-shirt with you."

"Looks like I'm not of the woods yet, does it?" I sighed. "I'll head over there, but if you haven't heard from me in an hour after you close your store, OK?"

"Great, that's how I want to spend my evening," Mandy said before hanging up.

It took me 20 minutes to reach the Speedway Police Department. After finding a parking spot, I rummaged through my laundry basket and found my Jeff Gordon T-shirt.

"Good, you're finally here," Detective Harrington said after greeting me in the station's lobby, "We need to put you in a police lineup."

"But what if I don't want to?"

"Then we'll arrest you for obstruction," the female officer standing next to the detective said firmly. "So, do we have your cooperation?"

I shrugged.

"Good," the female officer said. "Follow me. You'll need to put on your T-shirt."

Once I finished changing in the woman's restroom, Melissa Peterson, the female officer, stuck me in a room with five other blonds. All were wearing Jeff Gordon T-shirts. A minute later, Detective Harrington ordered each of us to step forward and slowly turn around so the witnesses behind the one-way window in front of us could see the back of our T-shirts.

When the lineup ended, Officer Peterson stepped back into the room.

"You can all go except Ms. DeCarlo," she said. "You'll need to stay behind."

"What's going on?" I said, raising my voice. "I didn't kill Fatso."

"Calm down ma'am," Peterson said. "One of the witnesses picked you out of the lineup, so we need to ask you some more questions. Let's find a smaller interrogation room."

As we stepped into the hallway, I looked up and spotted Mandy sitting on a wooden bench in the waiting room at the far end of the hall. I broke free of Officer Peterson's grip on my arm and ran toward Mandy.

"Tell this cop I didn't kill Lenny Walton," I said, bursting into tears.

Mandy put her arm around my shoulder and tried to console me as Officer Peterson caught up to us.

"Do that again, Ms. DeCarlo, and I'll put you in handcuffs," Peterson said, giving me a look that could kill. "Now, let's go."

"But officer, I didn't kill Lenny Walton. You've gotta believe me. That witness is lying."

"Witness?" Mandy said.

"Yeah, somebody picked me out of a lineup a few minutes ago."

"Were two of them the dorks that we ran into at the track yesterday?" Mandy asked.

"I don't know," I said. "Why?"

"'Cause I spotted them as I was walking into the station a few minutes ago. They were talking to some blond. From behind, she looked a lot like you."

"Molly Pollock," I said.

"Who's that?"

"Lenny's former girlfriend," I explained. "That's it. Lenny must have followed her into that restroom. And I'll bet you anything that she was wearing a T-shirt just like mine. Why else would he go after her?"

I turned to Officer Peterson, who now had a vise grip on my arm.

"Was Molly Pollock one of the witnesses?" I asked.

"I can't tell you that, but since your friend mentioned it, one of the witnesses did look a little like you," Peterson said.

"Let's put you and your friend in an interrogation room for a minute. I need to check on something."

Mandy and I sat on some uncomfortable metal chairs in an interrogation room for at least a half-hour before Officer Peterson returned.

"What's going on?" I asked.

"We contacted the witness that your friend saw, and she's agreed to return to the station. Tell me the name of Lenny Walton's girlfriend again?"

"Molly Pollock," I said. "She looks a little like me, only she's younger, according to Lenny's grandmother."

"Thanks," Officer Peterman said as she left the room. "I'll keep you posted."

"Think that witness was Molly Pollock?" Mandy asked after Peterson left.

"Absolutely," I replied. "What's the chance of those dorks knowing another woman at the track?"

"Good point."

An hour later, Peterson returned.

"Ms. DeCarlo, you and your friend, can leave now."

"I'm no longer a person of interest?"

"That's right, you're not," Peterson said.

"What's happened?"

"We're still waiting on Mr. Walton's autopsy, but Ms. Pollock has admitted to owning a Jeff Gordon T-shirt like yours and to being at the track on Sunday."

"See, I told you it had to be her."

Officer Peterson just smiled and escorted us to the front door of the station.

Two days later, I'd just stuck Lonnie Sparks' nails in a soapy solution when my cell phone went off inside my handbag.

"Is this a bad time, Candi?"

I glanced across my nail station at Lonnie and whispered that Martha Rae Folger was on the line. Lonnie nodded approvingly before sticking an iPod earplug in her ear.

"I'm working on Lonnie Sparks right now, but she says it's OK to talk to you for a few minutes."

"Great. Tell Lonnie I said, 'hi.' What a great lady. I hope I'm as bright as her when I'm 80," Martha Rae said, before adding, "I just read a news story out of Indianapolis that says Lenny Walton's girlfriend has been charged with his death. Something about them pushing each other in the woman's stall and him hitting his head against the toilet bowl. Looks like you're finally off the hook. Can I get your reaction once this commercial ends in five…four…two…and one second?

"Welcome back, folks," I heard Martha Rae tell her audience. "Candi DeCarlo is on the line. Best darn manicurist in town. So, if you need your nails done give her a call at Tips & Toes. But that's not why we're talking to her today. You probably heard about the guy who was found lying dead inside a woman's restroom at the Brickyard 400. Well, turns out Candi found him. The cops thought she'd killed the guy and were all set to lock her up and throw away the key. That is, until his girlfriend was charged with his death today. Candi, is that an accurate account of what happened?"

"Pretty much, Martha Rae," I said. "But I gotta tell you, I was really scared after I got picked out of the police lineup."

"This story says the police think Lenny Walton followed his former girlfriend into the restroom, but doesn't say why. Got any ideas?"

"I heard they just broke up, but I think the real reason is that she was wearing a Jeff Gordon T-shirt like mine."

"Why would anybody get mad about that?"

"Lenny was a huge Tony Stewart fan," I said. "And everybody knows Jeff and Tony don't always get along."

"Let me ask you another question," Martha Rae said. "Is it true what they say here? Did Lenny have a hot dog stuffed in his mouth?"

"Yup," I said. "Only a little bit of it was sticking out."

"Wow," Martha Rae said. "I guess I'll let you get back to Lonnie. I'm glad you're no longer a person of interest. And I'm sorry that you missed the finals of the Jeff Gordon contest. But you're a winner in my book."

A commercial began playing in the background before Martha Rae came back on the line.

"Thanks for the interview, Candi," she said. "I appreciate you not letting on about me knowing Lenny. My listeners don't need to know I used to babysit that jerk."

On Friday night, I trudged up the outside stairs that led to my second-story apartment. I was exhausted. It'd been a long week, but it still wasn't over. Judging from our appointment book, Saturday was going to be another busy day at Tips & Toes. All I wanted to do right now was take a warm bubble bath, munch on the Ho Ho's I'd just bought at the Grab & Run, and pour myself a diet Dr. Pepper.

As I neared the landing, I noticed a FedEx box leaning against my front door. What could that be?

I quickly unlocked the door and threw my groceries on the kitchen counter before retrieving the box. I then sat down on my couch and ripped the open end of it. A white envelope fell out. I picked it up off the floor and quickly opened it.

"Dear Candi," it began. "Your friend, Martha Rae Folger, told me how you ran into some trouble on your way to the finals of our contest. Sorry to hear that, but I understand everything's OK now. Hope you enjoy the little present inside. All the best. Jeff."

I reread the letter before glancing at the return address on the front of the box. Hendricks Racing Team. Charlotte, North Carolina.

"It's from Jeff Gordon," I screamed, as I tipped the box on its side. A red leather racing jacket fell out. I picked it up off the floor and quickly tried it on. It fit perfectly.

"I love you, Jeff Gordon," I shouted at the top of my lungs.

Originally published in the
Bedlam at the Brickyard Anthology, *Blue River Press, 2009.*

Catchin' Cooter

"It's him … it's really him."

"Him who?"

"Cooter Martin."

"Huh?"

For the past 45 minutes, me and my best friend, Mandy Malone, had been sitting at a tiny table at Rick's Hideaway Lounge, sipping strawberry daiquiris and checking out the scenery. Which wasn't much. At least not until Cooter Martin and his fine-looking booty walked through the front door and sat down at the bar.

"You never heard of Cooter?" I asked Mandy. "He was Dale's chief mechanic when he won the championship in '80."

"Whoopee do," Mandy said, twirling a finger in the air and sipping on her drink.

"How'd you know about him?"

"Bobby," I replied. "He made me sit on the couch and watch the stock car races. He liked to tell stories about NASCAR drivers and their mechanics."

"Too bad he didn`t use some of those brain cells to find a better job to help support you and your daughter."

I let out a long sigh, shoved my drink across the table and stood up.

"Where are you going?"

"To the bar," I said. "I want to see if it's really Cooter Martin or if I'm just dreaming."

Five minutes later, I dragged Cooter back to the table, along with two more strawberry daiquiris. Cooter was wearing a long-sleeved red shirt, faded jeans and some fancy lookin' cowboy boots. The cute little gray hairs peeking out from underneath his NASCAR ball cap made him look very distinguished.

"Mandy, this here's Cooter," I said.

Cooter winked and tipped the brim of his hat before shaking Mandy's hand.

"Pleased to make your acquaintance, ma'am," he said. "Any friend of Candi DeCarlo is a friend of mine."

"Whatever," Mandy said, grabbing one of the daiquiris out of my hands.

I glared at Mandy. I hate it when she acts that way in front of strangers. I`ve known her since kindergarten, but she`s become anti-social ever since her third husband took a dirt nap two years ago. Now, she spends her evenings taking bubble baths in her five-bedroom mansion. I practically had to hog tie her before she came out with me tonight.

"Is Cooter your real name?" Mandy asked, looking up from her drink.

"Yes ma'am. Daddy gave it to me after visiting momma in the hospital the day I was born. Nurses had wrapped me up real tight in a blanket. Only my head was peeking through when daddy laid eyes on me. Told momma I reminded him of a cooter. And that's how I got my name."

"Isn't that an adorable story?" I gushed.

"If you don't mind being named after a baby turtle," Mandy said, sucking on her straw. "What brings you to Bartonsville, Cooter?"

"Just passing through when I decided to pull off the high-way and grab myself a drink," he said, taking a gulp of his beer. "I'm headed to Indy for the Brickyard 400."

"Are you still on the race circuit?" I asked.

"No, no, I haven't raced in years," Cooter said, flicking his baby blues at me. "But I stay in touch with Junior. Make sure he's okay since his daddy died at Daytona. After I called Junior last week, he sent me some tickets and pit passes. This is my first time at the Brickyard."

"You're going to love it," I said. "The Speedway is huge. And it's lots of fun, ain't that right, Mandy?"

"Whatever you say, honey." Mandy turned away to watch the band warm up.

"Reckon I'd best get going," Cooter said. "Still got lots to do tonight before I get to Indy."

"Cooter, do me a favor before you leave," I said, tugging at his shirt sleeve. "Can I get a couple autographs?"

"Sure thing, Candi," he replied. "Got something for me to sign?"

I reached into my handbag and pulled out some appointment cards.

"What's this say?" Cooter said, holding one of my cards at arm's length. "A nail technician, huh? Well, I'll be. Candi, I never would have figured you for one of them gals."

I smiled proudly but heard a long sigh to my right. It was Mandy.

"How many autographs do you need?" Cooter asked.

"One for me, and one for my ex," I said. "Mandy, do you want one?"

"I'll pass."

Cooter signed two appointment cards and handed them back. He stuffed a third one in his shirt pocket.

"Can you do me another favor, Cooter?" I said, flashing him a big smile.

"Anything for you, Candi," he said, returning the smile. "You're such a cute little sugar pie. What is it?"

"How about a picture of us together?" I said. "My ex will die when he sees it. He'll never believe you were here in Bartonsville."

"Sure thing. Got a camera?"

"You bet," I said, reaching into my handbag and pulling out my cell phone. "Here Mandy, take our picture."

I handed the phone to Mandy and stood next to Cooter. He grabbed me around the waist and pulled me in real tight. For a second, I thought we would fall over.

When Mandy finished taking our picture, Cooter asked if I liked NASCAR.

"Sure do."

"Junior sent me extra tickets and passes. If you gals want them, they're yours."

"Wow! Thanks, Cooter," I said, grabbing the tickets before he changed his mind. "Maybe we'll see you at the race."

I reached over and planted a big kiss on his cheek. He squeezed me one more time before he winked, tipped his hat at Mandy and left the bar.

"Ain't he sweet, Mandy?" I said, still fondling the tickets.

"Yeah, as sweet as a rattlesnake."

Normally it's slow at Tips & Toes on Saturday afternoons. Most clients have their nails done in the morning so they can spend their afternoons shopping at Walmart. But not today. We were busy all day. Even Madge Parsons, our owner, applied a set of acrylics to an old client of hers. Madge just likes to plop down on her stool behind the front counter and collect the money.

At three o'clock, Mary Donovan walked through the front door. Mary's a dispatcher at the Bartonsville Police Department and the smartest woman I know in town. Most folks think she should be the police chief, but the old farts on the town council don't agree. They can't stand the thought of a woman running their town. That's why they went out recently and hired Dan Cobb. But I'll give them old farts some credit; Dan's a real dreamboat and he's single, too.

"What's up, Mary?" I asked as she sat down at my nail station.

"Got us a murder on our hands on Fletcher Street."

"That's horrible," I said as I stuck Mary's nails in some soapy water. "What happened?"

"Neighbors hadn't seen the victim for a few days, so one of them knocked on her door this morning. He smelled something foul, became suspicious, and tried the door. It was unlocked so he walked inside. Found the woman lying on her kitchen floor. A steak knife sticking out of her chest."

"OMG, who was it?"

"LuAnn Taylor."

"I don't know her."

"Not surprising. Nobody in town knows much about her," Mary said. "She moved here six months ago from somewhere down south. Neighbors say she was friendly enough but kept to herself."

"But somebody disliked her," I said.

It was just after nine on Sunday morning when I roared my F-150 up Mandy's circular driveway and leaned on the horn.

A perfect day for the Brickyard 400. Not a cloud in the sky and the TV weather guy was predicting temperatures in the low 80s by race time.

A minute later, Mandy stepped out of her front door and climbed into my truck. She was wearing a loose-fitting tan cotton dress, brown scandals and a wide-brimmed sun bonnet. I was wearing one of Bobby's old NASCAR T-shirts, some cutoff jean shorts and a pair of old sneakers I found at the bottom of my closet.

"Why do you insist on blasting your horn every time you show up?" Mandy said. "It's loud enough to wake the dead."

I laughed. "It's time your neighbors got up."

During our 40-minute drive from Bartonsville to Indianapolis, I reminisced about the good times we used to have at the Indy 500, hanging out in the infield snake pit. But Mandy didn't remember any of it. She must have amnesia like one of those soap actresses.

Once we reached the town of Speedway, I found the tiny old house where we used to park. The lecherous old guy who waved cars onto his front lawn wasn't there. A young Hispanic dude was there instead. He wanted to charge us twenty bucks, but I flashed him a big smile and he took fifteen.

"I can't believe I let you talk me into coming here," Mandy said as we made our way through to the track gates. "I hate being around sweaty people and engine fumes. Right now, I could be sitting under a shady tree in my backyard or taking a long bubble bath."

"I know, sweetie," I said, patting Mandy's arm. "You're such a good sport and true friend. But I couldn't let Cooter's tickets go to waste. Besides, it's my first NASCAR race in person. Bobby always promised he'd take me to Talladega, but he never did."

Our seats in the grandstand were just past turn two. Once we'd settled into them, I took off Bobby's T-shirt, exposing my pink bikini top. I then pulled some suntan lotion out of my bag.

"Will you do me the honors?" I said, passing the tube of suntan lotion to Mandy.

"Do I have a choice?"

"Not really."

The lotion sent a chill down my spine. But, by the time Mandy finished spritzing it on my back, the lotion felt very soothing. And I won't look like a giant red tomato tomorrow.

"Where you going?" I asked after Mandy stood and handed me back my tube of suntan lotion.

"To the restroom to wipe off this icky stuff," she said. "And then I'm going to buy some ear plugs. The noise is louder than I remember."

After Mandy left, I applied some lotion to my arms and face. I had just stretched out to enjoy the sun when I heard my cell phone ring. It plays the Star-Spangled Banner. I reached down and picked up my handbag.

"That you, Candi?"

It was Mary Donovan.

"Mandy and I are at the Brickyard 400 and the race is about to begin."

"I won't keep you, but I've got a quick question," Mary said. "Didn't you tell me yesterday that you didn't know LuAnn Taylor?"

"That's the gal who was stabbed to death, right? Nope, I never met her."

"Well, she apparently knew you."

"What do you mean, Mary?"

"The detectives found one of your appointment cards lying on the floor in her bedroom."

"I have no idea how it got there. Like I said before, I didn't know her."

Then it hit me. "Anything written on the front of the card?"

"I don't know," Mary replied. "Let me ask the Chief."

While Mary went off to find Chief Cobb, I quickly reviewed the situation. Mary told me yesterday that LuAnn Taylor moved here from somewhere down south. Cooter Martin lives in South Carolina. And I remember Cooter saying he had lots to do before going to Indy. What if one of those things was stabbing LuAnn Taylor, but why? My mind was going as fast as the cars doing their warmups around the track when Mary came back on line.

"The Chief says there's nothing written on the front of your card."

"Hmmm," I said.

"Is there something you're not telling me?"

"I don't know yet, Mary. I'll call you back."

I threw my phone back in my bag and stood up as Mandy returned to our seats.

"Where are you going?" she asked.

"To look for Cooter in the pits."

"Why, for God sakes?"

I quickly filled Mandy in on my conversation with Mary, and how Cooter stuck one of my appointment cards in his shirt pocket at the bar on Friday night.

"So what?" she replied. "You don't think Cooter stabbed that woman, do you?"

"I don't want to believe it. Cooter seems too sweet to do anything like that, but I need to find out if he's still got my card. Want to come with me?"

"No thanks," she said. "I don't want some grease monkey spilling oil on my Egyptian cotton dress. I paid a lot for it."

"Suit yourself."

It took me 20 minutes to weave my way through the crowd and reach the pit area. A burly looking rent-a-cop stood in front of the entrance checking people's passes. I fished around in my bag looking for mine. It was hiding underneath my makeup kit. Once inside the pits, I wasn't sure where Cooter could be, so I began wandering around looking for him. I got lucky. Less than five minutes later, I literally ran into him.

"What are you doing here?" Cooter asked with a surprised look on his face.

"Duh, don't you remember? You gave me and Mandy tickets and passes on Friday night."

"Oh, yeah, I forgot. Say, I'd love to stay and chat, but I need to get going."

Just then, I looked up and spotted two cops jogging toward us. They were fifty feet away.

"Hold it right there, Martin," one of them shouted.

I glanced at Cooter. He had a panicked look on his face.

"Come here, Candi," he said as the cops drew closer.

"Huh?"

When I didn't move, Cooter reached out and grabbed my arm and pulled me close. He then reached in his pants pocket and pulled out a switchblade and put it near my throat.

"What are you doing, Cooter?" I screamed.

"Relax, Candi. I don't want to hurt you, but you're my ticket out of here."

"Drop the knife, Martin, and let that woman go," the shorter of the two cops shouted. They were now less than six feet away with their guns drawn.

"Put your guns away, boys, or I'll slit Candi's throat."

"Do what he says," I pleaded. "I'm a grandma, but I'm too young to die."

The cops stopped in their tracks, but their guns were still pointed at us.

"Too bad they didn't listen to you, Candi," Cooter said to me. "Now, start backing up so I can get out of here."

"You stabbed that woman, didn't you, Cooter?"

"Shut up, Candi."

"And these cops know it."

"I said shut up, or I'll stab you, too."

Cooter grabbed me around the waist and began dragging me backwards. As he did, I pulled my bag up to my chest. With my right hand, I reached inside and carefully unscrewed the top to the tube of suntan lotion.

"How much longer are we going to do this?" I asked Cooter.

"Until we get beyond the pit gate and I can make a run for it."

"Are we there yet? I'm not used to walking backwards."

"I told you to shut up, Candi. Keep walking or I'll stab you."

Cooter then pricked my neck with the tip of his knife.

That did it. I let out a blood curdling scream. Cooter let go of my waist long enough for me to pull the suntan lotion completely out of my bag, turn and squirt him in the face.

He dropped the knife and began rubbing his eyes with both hands. When the cops realized what happened, they charged forward, shoved me aside, threw Cooter to the ground and quickly handcuffed him. A minute later, one of the cops returned to help me to my feet.

"Are you okay, ma`am?" he asked. "That was a very foolish thing you did. He could have slit your throat."

"I know."

Within minutes, the place was swarming with more cops and local TV camera crews. A middle-aged detective in a bad toupee took my statement before letting me go.

On my way back to the grandstand, my cell phone went off. It must be Mandy wondering where I am.

"Are you okay, Candi?" Mary Donovan asked. "I figured you were holding back on me when we talked before, so I mentioned it to Chief Cobb. He told me about talking to LuAnn Taylor's relatives yesterday and learning she was Cooter Martin's sister-in-law. She blamed Cooter for her sister's mysterious death and thought he murdered her for insurance money. LuAnn's relatives also told the Chief that Cooter was headed to Indy for the Brickyard 400. We began putting it all together, but the Chief and I couldn't figure out how you may have met Cooter."

"He stopped by Rick's for a beer on Friday night. Me and Mandy ended up talking to him. Cooter signed a couple of my appointment cards and put an extra one in his shirt pocket."

"So that's why you acted so strangely when I asked about your appointment card?" Mary said.

"Figured it must have been something like that. Anyway, the Chief called his old pals at the Indianapolis Metropolitan Police Department. Said Cooter was the prime suspect in LuAnn Taylor's death. And told them to look for him at the track."

I told Mary I needed to get off the phone and find Mandy. I hadn't seen her in nearly an hour. She was probably worried about me. But I promised Mary I'd swing by the station on my way home and tell her all the gory details of Cooter holding me hostage at knife point.

Mandy was sitting quietly in her seat watching the race when I finally made it back to the grandstand.

"Are you okay?" I asked.

"I'm fine," she said. "You've missed a terrific race so far. I didn't realize NASCAR races could be so much fun. By the way, where have you been?"

I smiled. "I'll tell you later."

Rescuing My Ex

George Clooney and I were walking along a deserted beach somewhere in the Caribbean when I heard my ringtone go off.

No, not now, I said slowly rolling out of bed and grabbing my cell phone off the nightstand. My clock radio said it was 3:45 a.m.

"Hello?"

"Is that you, Candi?"

"No, it's Julia Roberts. What do you want, Bobby?"

Bobby DeCarlo is my ex. We've been divorced more than two years, but he still calls me at all hours of the day and night.

"I'm in trouble," Bobby said.

"What have you done now?"

"I'm not sure. Nathan Sloan and Frank Turner showed up on my doorstep a half hour ago and arrested me. We're on our way to the police station. They let me use my cell to make my one call."

"What do you want from me?"

"Can you bail me out of jail? You know I'm afraid of spending the night there."

♥ ♥ ♥

It took fifteen minutes before I arrived at the Bartonsville Police Station. Mary Donovan, the department's night dispatcher, was perched on a stool behind a plexiglass window as I walked through the station's side door.

"What are you doing here, Candi?" she asked. "I thought you and Bobby were divorced."

"We are, but he's terrified of being locked up," I said. "He got scared straight while on a high school field trip to the state prison. I'm here to bail him out."

"Ain't going to happen, darlin.' He's accused of stabbing a guy to death with a six-inch long hunting knife in the parking lot of Rick's Hideaway Lounge."

"What? Bobby killed someone?" I said, as I felt my legs go limp. "That's impossible. Bobby doesn't own a hunting knife. The only hunting he does is hunting women."

"Maybe so, but at least four guys in the parking lot identified him as the perpetrator. The victim died in an ambulance on the way to the hospital."

"I can't believe it," I said. "Bobby's a real jerk most of the time, but he's never killed anyone, and not with a knife. Who's the dead guy?"

"Can't say," Mary said. "His next of kin haven't been notified."

♥ ♥ ♥

"What's with you?" Joanie Sullivan asked as I trudged through the door to Ralph's Diner an hour later and plopped down on a stool at the lunch counter. "You look like hell. Want your usual?"

"No, just give me some coffee," I replied, trying to keep my head from hitting the counter top. "Lots of black coffee."

A minute later, Joanie set a coffee mug in front of me. "So, what's wrong this morning?"

"Bobby's been arrested for murder," I said after taking a giant swig of my coffee.

"What!" Joanie shouted. "Bobby DeCarlo is a murderer!"

"I know. It's like a nightmare that has become true."

"It doesn't sound like the Bobby I know," Joanie said. "Isn't he all talk and no action? A lover instead of a fighter. He acted that way when he'd wander in here before you were divorced."

"You're right, Joanie. Bobby prefers chasing women to fighting with someone. The cops got it all wrong. He couldn't have stabbed anyone."

"Have you told Jenny yet?"

"No, I didn't want to wake her this early." Jenny is my daughter. Bobby and I had her during my junior year in high school. She's married now and has two kids of her own, Jacob and Abby.

"You'll need to tell her sooner or later," Joannie said. "You don't want her to hear about the murder on some Indianapolis TV station."

"I know. I'll call her later this morning."

"What are you going to do in the meantime?"

"Drink more coffee and find a way to prove Bobby's innocence."

Tips & Toes didn't have any clients when I entered the salon a half hour later. My co-worker, Trudy Castle, said our boss, Madge Parsons, wouldn't arrive until noon. She'd stayed overnight again at one of the casino boats along the Ohio River.

I picked up my cell to call Jenny, but put it back in my handbag. She was probably busy getting the grandkids ready for school. I'll call her later. No sense putting any more strain on our mother-daughter relationship.

It was closer to one o'clock when Madge entered the salon and headed straight to my nail station.

"I heard the news about Bobby on WYMN," she said. "Why would he murder someone?"

"What makes you so sure he did?"

"I dunno. You're divorced. He probably threatened you in the past; otherwise, you'd still be married to him."

"No, Madge, Bobby never threatened me. His problem was other women. He liked them more than he liked me."

"Oh," Madge said. "I'm sorry. I didn't know. You've never really told me much about your personal life before today."

"Madge, can I leave early so I can find out what happened to him last night?"

"Of course, honey," Madge said. "Leave now if you'd like. It's probably just as well. You won't get anything done here if clients keep asking you about your ex."

It took me ten minutes to straighten up my nail station before leaving. I jumped into my Ford F-150 parked behind the salon and headed to the scene of last night's crime.

Rick Ives, the owner of Rick's Hideaway Lounge, was wiping down some freshly washed glasses when I walked into his place. It was deserted except for an old guy bent over his beer at the far end of the bar.

"Here to learn what happened last night?" Rick asked when he spotted me. "Can I fix you a drink first? You look like you could use one."

"No, water will be fine," I replied. "So, what did happen?"

"Wish I knew," Rick said, placing a glass of water in front of me. "We were real busy last night. One of my girls called in sick. Bobby and Phil Butler got into it with some dudes over using the pool table. Things got heated so I told Bobby and the others to take it outside. Next thing I know the parking lot was lit up like a Christmas tree with cop cars everywhere."

"Who was stabbed?"

"Don't know. Chief Cobb said the guy and his motorcycle buddies were from Indianapolis. He's still tracking down the victim's relatives the last I heard."

"Big city boys, eh?" I said, taking a swig of water.

"Yeah, they were a tough-looking crew," Rick said.

"I saw the whole thing." It was the old guy at the end of the bar.

I glanced at him and then back at Rick. He shrugged as I stood up and wandered over to the old guy.

"What did you see, sir?" I asked, sitting down next to him.

"Call me Charlie," the guy said, shaking my hand. "Tell you the truth, I could probably think a whole lot better if I had another beer in my hand."

I motioned to Rick, who dropped a beer in front of Charlie and walked away.

"Okay, sir, what did you see last night?" I asked.

"It was like Rick said. Bobby got into an argument with these guys at the pool table. Rick told them to take a walk and they did."

"Did you go outside?"

"Of course, but not before I finished my beer. You can't leave a full beer lying around here anymore. Somebody's liable to walk off with it, or worse, the bartender will throw it away."

"What did you see?"

"Bobby had a hunting knife. He lunged at this guy, who fell to the ground. Everybody scattered and pretty soon every cop in town showed up."

"How'd you know it was Bobby?"

"I'd recognize him anywhere. He was wearing his high school varsity jacket. That boy was a helluva quarterback in his day. Too bad he broke his leg in his senior year and didn't win a college scholarship. He could have made it all the way to the NFL."

"Anything else?" I asked.

"Nope, but I'm all out of beer," Charlie said.

Rather than buy him another, I thanked Charlie for his time and quickly left the bar. Before driving away, I called my best friend, Mandy Malone. She picked up on the second ring.

"Where are you?" I asked.

"Driving home from Indy," she said. "Remember, I was at an all-day business conference. I heard about Bobby on the radio. How are you holding up?"

"I've been up since before four," I said. "I just talked to Rick and an old guy named Charlie. I'm convinced Bobby didn't do it. Did your conference get over early?"

"No, the speakers were boring, so I left," Mandy said. "Taking a bubble bath at home seemed like a better use of my time. So, what are you doing next?"

"I thought I'd stop by Phil Butler's place," I said. "Rick said he and Bobby were together last night."

"Have you called Jenny?"

"No, I haven't had time," I said. "Joanie said I should call her before she hears about it on the evening news."

"Joanie's right," Mandy replied. "Why don't you let me do it. She's liable to be less upset if she hears about her daddy from her favorite auntie. Go see Phil."

♥ ♥ ♥

Phil Butler was Bobby's favorite wide receiver in high school. Both broke several school records. And, both had early college scholarship offers, but after Bobby broke his leg, the offers dried up. Phil ended up at a small private college in Illinois but came home after his freshman year. Said he was homesick, so he went to work at his dad's welding shop.

As I pulled into the parking lot of Butler & Son Welding, I spotted Phil standing at the front door. He appeared to be locking up early.

"Hey, Candi, what are you doing here?" Phil said as he watched me step out of my truck.

"Heard you and Bobby got into a fight last night?"

"Guess you could call it that," Phil said, rubbing the back of his head. "Me and Bobby were playing pool when these dudes tried to take the table away from us. Bobby mouthed off to them, and the next thing I knew, we were all rolling around in the parking lot."

"Did you see Bobby knife anybody?"

"Not really," Phil said. "Some big fat dude jumped me once we were outside. He threw me to the ground and sat on me. He had bad breath and wouldn't let me up."

"An old guy I met at the bar today said Bobby lunged at the victim with a hunting knife. Bobby doesn't own one, does he?"

"Beats me," Phil said. "I've never seen him with one. You know Bobby. He tells everybody he's a lover, not a fighter."

"The old guy recognized Bobby because he was wearing his varsity jacket."

"Doubt that."

"What do you mean?"

"We took off our jackets when we were playing pool and didn't have time to pick them up before Rick threw us out of his place."

❤ ❤ ❤

"Good evening. Bartonsville Police Department. How can we help you?"

"Mary, it's me. Candi. How's Bobby doing today?"

"Better than last night," Mary replied. "He went through a box of tissues, crying like a baby. He finally fell asleep from sheer exhaustion."

"Amazing," I said. "I only saw Bobby cry once before. It was the day Judge Stone ordered him to turn his truck over to me at our divorce hearing. What's going to happen to him now?"

"The detectives are still talking to witnesses, but Chief Cobb and the county prosecutor will need to charge Bobby by tomorrow or let him go."

"They still think he murdered the guy?"

"Yeah, I'm afraid so. The knife was lying next to Bobby when the first officers showed up. We're waiting to see if his fingerprints were on the knife handle."

"Mary, I learned something this afternoon that makes me think Bobby didn't murder anyone."

"What are you talking about?"

"Phil Butler says Bobby wasn't wearing his varsity jacket during the scuffle in the parking lot, but an old guy at the Hideaway swears he had it on."

"Wait a minute. You think someone set Bobby up to make it look like he committed the crime?"

"Yup."

"That changes everything," Mary said. "Let me talk to Chief Cobb. He'll want to know about this right away."

I'd been home only a half hour when I heard my doorbell ring. I peeked through the curtain covering the top half of my front door. I thought it might be Mandy telling me about her conversation with Jenny, but, instead, it was Chief Dan Cobb.

"What are you doing here?" I asked after opening my door.

"Mary says you have some new information about the stabbing last night."

"Maybe," I said, directing the Chief to sit in the big stuffed chair in my living room. I sat in my rocking chair and told him what I'd learned from talking to Phil Butler and Charlie, the old guy at the bar.

"Butler didn't mention anything about Bobby's jacket when I interviewed him earlier today," Chief Cobb said.

"Knowing Phil, he probably doesn't remember too much about last night. He and Bobby tend to drink too much when they're together."

"Who's this Charlie guy?"

"Never asked him his last name, but Rick will know it," I replied. "He appears to be a regular there."

"I'll get back to you," the Chief said as he stood and left my apartment.

The next morning, I met Mandy for breakfast at Ralph's Diner. She called me after Chief Cobb left last night. I figured she wasn't satisfied with our brief phone call yesterday afternoon. Mandy always likes to know what's going on in town. Besides, I needed to find out about her call to Jenny. Was my daughter mad at me for not calling her myself?

As Mandy and I walked through Ralph's front door, I stopped dead in my tracks.

"What's wrong?" Mandy asked as she almost bumped into me.

"Look," I said, pointing to a guy sitting at the lunch counter. "It's Bobby. He's wearing his varsity jacket. He's been freed."

With that, I rushed over to my ex and gave him a big bear hug from behind.

"Hey, lady, what are you doing?" the guy said as he swiveled around on his stool.

"You're not Bobby," I shouted.

"No, but I can be," he said, giving me a smarmy look.

I punched his arm and demanded to know why he was wearing Bobby's jacket.

"I found it in the dumpster behind the Hideaway," the guy replied. "It's a perfectly good jacket. I don't know why anyone would throw it away."

"Take it off, mister," Mandy said. "It's evidence in a murder."

"Huh?" the guy replied.

"You heard me. Take it off, or I'll blast you with my pepper spray." She had taken it out of her handbag.

I jumped between Mandy and the guy before she followed through on her threat. The guy could see Mandy wasn't about to put away her pepper spray, so he slowly took off the jacket.

"What should we do now?" I asked Mandy.

"Call the cops and tell them to send someone here right away. Meanwhile, I'll keep my spray aimed on this guy in case he decides to make a run for it."

Ten minutes later, Chief Cobb walked into Ralph's.

"What's going on?" he asked.

"We've captured the slasher from the Hideaway," Mandy said, finally putting away her pepper spray.

"Let me be the judge of that," Chief Cobb replied, grabbing Bobby's jacket and the guy by the arm before they left the diner.

♥ ♥ ♥

It was nearing six o'clock when I finished some French nails for my last client of the day and left the salon. I planned to drive by the Grab & Run first for a package of Ho Ho's and liter of Diet Dr. Pepper. Instead, I decided to treat myself to dinner at Ralph's. After all, I'd ended up with several good tips today. People must have been feeling sorry for me.

As I entered the diner, the guy wearing Bobby's varsity jacket was sitting at the counter again. I rushed toward him, punched him in the back and shouted, "Give me that jacket, mister!"

"What are you doing, Candi?" Bobby said after spinning around on his stool.

"Bobby, it's you," I replied. "What are you doing here? I thought you were still in jail. You got your jacket back."

"It isn't my jacket. It belongs to Phil. The cops are keeping mine as evidence. About an hour ago, Chief Cobb let me go. They arrested a guy for the murder the other night. Phil picked me up and drove me here."

"Who was the murderer?"

"The Chief told me his name, but I can't remember it. He was one of the dudes fighting with me and Phil.

"I don't understand."

"Seems the guy had a knife and accused his buddy of messing with his girlfriend. When Rick threw us outside, he grabbed my jacket, put it on, stabbed his friend, and then threw my jacket in Rick's dumpster before fleeing on his motorcycle."

"So, that's why Charlie and the other witnesses thought you stabbed the guy, but it wasn't you at all."

"Candi, you should know by now I'm a lover, not a fighter," Bobby said, patting the top of the stool next to him. "Sit down here, let's have dinner and talk about the good old days?"

"No, I'm going home," I said. "I need to call Jenny and let her know that you're okay, but do me a favor, Bobby? Don't call me again in the middle of the night."

"But, Candi…"

Mom's Prince Charming

Trudy Castle slowly opened the door to our storage room and stuck her head inside. "Candi, there's a woman out here asking for you."

"Can't you give her a manicure?" I replied. "I'm still busy laundering and folding the towels we use for our pedicure clients."

"I can, but the woman insists on talking to you."

"Who is she?"

"She didn't say, but I have a feeling she's related to you."

Trudy must be testing her psychic powers again.

"Okay," I said. "Do me a favor? Finish folding these towels and pull the final load out of the dryer. I'll find out what the woman wants."

As I stepped out of the storage room, I realized Trudy had been right. I was related to the woman standing at the front counter. It was my mother, Wanda Mae Thompson.

"What are you doing here?" I asked, still in shock at seeing her after nearly two years.

"Can't I drop by and say hello to my only daughter?" Mom replied before stepping forward and giving me a huge hug.

Whew! I forgot how Mom's cheap perfume makes me nauseous. It's worse than Madge's.

"How'd you know I worked here?" I said, stepping back to grab a breath of fresh air.

"The folks at Ralph's Diner said you no longer worked there, and I could find you here."

"So, what do you want?"

"Now, Candi, don't be so snarky. I know I'm not the Mother of the Year type, but I do think about you from time to time and wonder how you're doing."

"Thanks, Mom," I said, trying not to snicker. "It's nice to know you haven't completely forgotten me. So, what brings you in here today?"

"I'm getting married."

"What? You're getting married? You've never done that before."

"I know, honey. I truly loved your father, but he left town the minute I told him that I was pregnant with you. Your stepbrother's father seemed more the marrying type until I learned he was on his way to prison for stabbing someone. But, now, I've found the man of my dreams."

"Who is the lucky fellow?"

"Clarence Woods. He's a widower who lives in a beautiful ranch house in Speedway near the racetrack. He once owned a small chain of Blockbuster video stores."

"Wow, he definitely sounds more stable than your other suitors. Congratulations. Sounds like you've finally found your Prince Charming," I said, trying to sound upbeat. "Where did you meet Clarence?"

"At the St. Christopher's bingo game in Speedway. My girlfriend, Suzy, and I dropped by one night three months ago. Clarence happened to sit next to us and, as they say, one thing led to another. I moved in with him two months ago."

"What about your double-wide at the Shady Pines Mobile Home Park?"

"It's a long story. I don't own it anymore. I fell behind on my rent. Charlie Taylor, the park manager, took me to small claims court where some nasty old judge ordered it repossessed."

"I'm sorry to hear it," I said, surprised that Mom hadn't called to borrow rent money from me. She had done it before.

"It's water under the bridge now that I've met Clarence," Mom replied. "He's already bought plane tickets for our honeymoon trip to Hawaii. But it's not why I stopped. I want you to be my Maid of Honor."

"Your Maid of Honor?" I said, trying not to faint in front of her. What should I say? I hummed and hawed for a minute before finally saying, "Can I get back to you in a day or so?"

"Fair enough. And, while you're at it, see if my beautiful great granddaughter, Abby, wants to be my flower girl?"

"I'm sure she'll love to do it," I replied.

"Listen, Candi, I need to run. I promised Clarence I'd be home early to fix him a pot roast for dinner. It's his favorite.

I'll call in a few days to get your answer and tell you when and where the wedding will take place."

Mom blew me an air kiss, quickly turned and left the nail salon.

"The laundry is finished," Trudy said a moment later. "By the way, who was that woman you were talking to?"

"My mother," I replied. "She's getting married."

"Wow. That's exciting news, but isn't she a little old to be a bride?"

"Tell me about it."

Madge Parsons, the owner of Tips & Toes, called a half hour later to say her annual physical was taking longer than usual, and she wouldn't be returning to work today. We didn't have another appointment in our book, so I told Trudy that she could leave early. I'd drop off our night deposit at the State Bank of Bartonsville.

Once Trudy left, I called Mandy Malone. She's been my best friend since kindergarten.

"What's up?" Mandy asked after picking up her phone.

"I had an unexpected visitor today."

"Who?"

"My mother."

"No kidding. What did Wanda Mae want?"

"She's getting married."

"What? Your mother has finally found some poor sucker to marry her. Who says wonders never cease?"

"I can't believe it either. Finding Mr. Right after years of a steady stream of 'uncles' showing up on our doorstep and staying with us for a few months. I'm still trying to process it. Can we get together and talk about it? If not, I need to find myself a shrink."

"I'll meet you for dinner at six, but you're buying. My listening services aren't free."

♥ ♥ ♥

Mandy was ten minutes late showing up at Ralph's Diner. Like me, she's usually very punctual. She said something about receiving a phone call on her way that kept her from being on time, but she didn't say who called.

We quickly ordered dinner. Mandy had a Cobb salad with vinaigrette dressing on the side. I tried the meatloaf special. It came with mashed potatoes, brown gravy, green beans, and apple pie a la mode for dessert. I eat more when I'm upset.

"So, tell me all about Wanda Mae's Prince Charming?" Mandy asked as she slid her salad around on her plate. She hates being last to learn about the current gossip in town.

I told her how Clarence Woods was a successful former video store entrepreneur who owned his own home in Speedway.

"Sounds like Wanda Mae won't need to borrow any more money from you," Mandy said when I finished.

"Tell me about it. When I was a teenager, she'd take my babysitting money to help pay the rent on our double wide. She also never attended my music recitals on time. And, Mom never held a job very long because she couldn't crawl out of bed on time in the mornings. It's a wonder I didn't end up in therapy after all that."

"Look at it this way," Mandy said when I finished venting. "She's now Clarence's problem."

"You're right," I said, smiling and clinking my glass of Diet Dr. Pepper with Mandy's sweet tea. "I'm curious. Who called on your way here?"

"Wanda Mae."

"How did she have your cell number?"

"I must have given it to her sometime in the past. I don't recall."

"Did she invite you to her wedding?" I asked.

"Actually, she asked if she could have her wedding at my place."

"What?"

"She said Clarence would be impressed when he learned she knew a rich person in Bartonsville. That's me."

"What did you tell her?" I asked.

"I'd think about it."

"You can't be serious."

"I wasn't at first, but if I hosted her wedding, the money I'd make could pay for the renovations I want to make to my McMansion. It could be a win-win."

"What would you charge her?"

"I don't know. It'll be Clarence's money, but I'll give her a deep discount. She's your mother, after all."

"Will you let Wanda Mae and Clarence spend their wedding night in one of your five bedrooms?"

"Eewww!"

♥ ♥ ♥

A few days later Mandy called to ask if I'd heard from my mother. Mandy also had found a woman who wanted to rent her place for a surprise birthday party. Mandy wouldn't commit to her until she knew my mother's plans.

"No, I haven't heard from her," I replied. "We've been so busy at work I completely spaced Mom's wedding. Let me call her and see what's up."

"Here's the number Wanda Mae gave me," Mandy said. "It's Clarence's landline. Let me know ASAP if she has picked a date. I don't want to lose out on the surprise birthday party gig."

Once Mandy hung up, I dialed Clarence's number. The phone rang four or five times before someone picked up.

"Is that you, Mom?"

"Yes," she replied in a low voice.

"Are you okay?"

"No."

"What's wrong?"

"Clarence left me for Donna Drew."

"Who is she?"

"Donna lives down the street from Clarence's place. He dated her for a short time after his wife died, but told me that he didn't care for her anymore. I was his one true love."

"How do you know Clarence and Donna ran off together?"

"I found a note on the kitchen table when I came home after shopping all day for my wedding dress. Clarence said he was sorry about everything. He didn't realize how much Donna meant to him until after I moved in. They left this afternoon for two weeks in Hawaii."

"Is that all he said?"

"No, he asked me to leave my set of house keys on the table. Clarence said it would be best if I wasn't here when he and Donna returned from Hawaii. What am I going to do, Candi? I'm now homeless."

I didn't know how to react to Mom's comment. In all the years we had lived together, I never remembered a time when we were evicted. We came close a few times, but Mom always managed to scrape together enough money to pay our rent, even if it meant raiding my piggy bank.

"I guess you could move in with me until you find a place of your own," I finally replied.

"Candi, you're a lifesaver. I had visions of ending up in a homeless shelter. How humiliating. I won't be any bother. How soon can you move me?"

"What did you have in mind?" I asked.

"How about tonight. I can't stand the thought of staying here another minute. Knowing Clarence is lying on some sandy beach in Hawaii with that gold digger, Donna Drew. It makes me sick to my stomach. I need to leave right now."

I hung up on my mother, but not before promising to stop by Clarence's house within the hour to load her stuff into my truck. Before leaving, I called Mandy to see if she could help. Her phone rang four or five times before it went to voice mail. Mandy was probably enjoying her nightly bubble bath. She refuses to do anything when she's soaking.

♥ ♥ ♥

Moving Mom nearly killed me. Who knew she had so many knick-knacks?

It wasn't that her boxes of stuff were too heavy to carry. It was the twenty steps leading to my second-floor apartment. After managing to carry the smallest box upstairs, Mom informed me that she couldn't help anymore.

"I'm having chest pains," she said, plopping down in my rocking chair. "I can't breathe. Honey, you'll need to carry the other boxes upstairs."

Thirteen boxes later, Mom was now officially moved in. When I asked what was inside her boxes, she replied that they were full of valuable keepsakes.

"I have some medals you won for your singing accomplishments in high school," she said. However, Mom never offered to let me see them. For the next two weeks, the boxes remained in the middle of my living room until I came home one night and dragged them into my daughter's old bedroom where Mom now slept.

Fixing dinner was awkward at first. When I lived alone, I often stopped by the Grab & Run convenience store after work to pick up a liter of Diet Dr. Pepper and a package of Ho Ho's for dinner. Obviously, that wouldn't work for Mom.

During our first week together, I'd rush home and fix Mac and Cheese with hot dogs or a meal of Hamburger Helper.

Mom soon became tired of my culinary choices. Midway through the second week, she called me at work and dictated a list of dinner items to pick up at the IGA store before coming home. She never offered to pick up the groceries herself. She hated leaving my place because of the outside steps

It was usually eight o'clock before Mom put dinner on the table, but it was delicious. I worried I was gaining weight and would no longer fit into my closet full of miniskirts or black pants.

One night I came home, not to a pot roast, but a bowl of Mac and Cheese.

"I spent most of the day looking for another place to live and didn't get home until an hour ago," Mom said, handing me my dinner.

"Have any luck?"

"I'll know in a day or so."

After dinner, Mom and I settled in to watch TV. An hour later, she asked if I had any popcorn.

"There's a package in the cupboard," I said. "Want some?"

I microwaved the popcorn and handed Mom a bowl. As we munched on our popcorn, Mom informed me she was giving up looking for another Prince Charming.

"You, on the other hand, had a Prince Charming and let him slip through your fingers."

"Who are you talking about?"

"Your ex-husband, Bobby DeCarlo."

"Bobby was hardly my Prince Charming," I said. "More like my charming philanderer."

"That's where you're wrong. Remember when Jennifer developed a high fever and you spent three or four days with her at the Riley Hospital for Children in Indianapolis?

"It was the worse days of my life. I thought I'd lose her. But, what does that have to do with Bobby? He never showed up at the hospital."

"He was working overtime on a construction job at the time. He'd stop by my place every night to ask about you and Jennifer. And, he'd start crying when I gave him the latest news. Bobby said he would never be able forgive himself if anything happened to your daughter."

"That's very touching, but it doesn't sound like the Bobby DeCarlo I know."

"If you don't believe me, ask him yourself."

When Mom finished her bowl of popcorn, she stood up and went to bed.

♥ ♥ ♥

Two days later, I came home early from work. After opening the front door, I shouted Mom's name, but she wasn't there. After putting my handbag down on the kitchen counter, I noticed a note.

"Dear Candi," it began. "A male admirer asked me to move in with him today. Charlie Taylor felt bad about repossessing my double wide. He became visibly upset when I told him how Clarence Woods treated me. Believe me, Charlie's no Prince Charming, but he genuinely likes me, and, at my age, I can't afford to ignore his affections. He came by this afternoon and moved my boxes to his place. Thanks for letting me stay with you. And, remember what I told you the other night. Don't stop looking for your own Prince Charming. Love Mom. P.S. Bobby deserves another chance."

I put down Mom's note, poured myself a glass of Diet Dr. Pepper and sat down in front of the TV with a package of Ho Ho's. Over the next three hours, I tried to concentrate on the shows on the TV, but kept thinking about Mom's note.

As I laid in bed later hugging my daughter's old teddy bear, Freddy, I couldn't get Mom's note out of my head. Telling me not to stop looking for my own Prince Charming. I wish it was that simple. And, what she said about Bobby. Had I really misjudged him?

"What should I do, Freddy?"

He didn't respond before I fell asleep.

No Love in the Tub

"What are we doing here, Candi?"

Mandy had a point. We'd just driven an hour over several back roads to end up in front of a tiny frame house near Loogootee, Indiana.

"I already told you," I said, glaring at Mandy as we walked up to the front door. "Patsy Slocum came to me in a dream last night. Told me she was murdered in her hot tub. Only I got scared and woke up before she could tell me who did it. But, I'm determined to find out now."

"I never liked Patsy," Mandy replied. "Miss I'm-better-than-everybody-else. Just because her daddy owned the only car dealership in town and she could drive any car she wanted around town."

"Stop whining," I said as I rapped on the front door. "Patsy was always nice to me. We were in glee club together. She once loaned me a prom gown when I competed in the Miss Fall Foliage contest."

"Who are you two?"

Mandy and I turned sideways. A Roseann Barr look-a-like dressed in a paisley caftan was leaning against the open doorway, her arms folded across her double D's. A freshly lit cigarette dangled from her lips.

"We're looking for Madame Filina. Psychic Extraordinaire," I said, pointing back to the tiny sign on the front yard.

"You got her," the woman snarled. "What do ya want?"

Great, a psychic with PMS instead of ESP.

"I'm Candi DeCarlo. Me and my friend here, Mandy Malone, want you to contact our friend, Patsy Slocum. She turned up face down in her hot tub a few days ago. The cops think she drowned from drinking too much. That's hogwash. Patsy could hold her liquor better than most men I know."

Madame Filina continued staring at us for another second or two before a tiny smile formed on her face. "Come in, ladies. Don't mind the mess. I wasn't expecting any clients today."

Mandy and I followed Filina down a dimly lit hallway littered with green garbage bags and walked into an even darker room. Once my eyes adjusted to the surroundings, I could see the room was about the size of a kid's bedroom. Filina lit a small candle in the middle of a rickety looking card table before she ordered me and Mandy to sit down on a pair of folding chairs.

"I charge thirty bucks to contact the dead," she said.

"No problem," I replied, reaching into my handbag and pulling out three tens.

Filina grabbed the money and quickly stuff it in her booby bank. She began the séance by asking us several questions about Patsy before she began chanting. It sounded like gibberish. But then I felt this whiff of air above me. Either Filina's AC just kicked in, or Patsy's spirit had decided to show up. It scared the be Jesus out of me and I shrieked.

"Shhh," Filina said. "Your friend is getting ready to speak."

Sure enough, a moment later, I heard someone or something whisper the name "Ray" two or three times. It gave me the willies.

I glanced at Mandy. She had the same look on her face she did that time we snuck into the Barton County Drive-in to see the Texas Chain Saw Massacre. Filina sat motionlessly in the folding chair, her eyes shut, and chubby arms dangling down at her side.

"Think she's okay?" I asked Mandy.

"I don't know. Feel her arm or something."

"I'm not touching her. You touch her."

A minute later, Filina leaned forward as though nothing happened and brought both of her elbows to rest on the table.

"Did you hear her?" she grinned. "Your friend Patsy called out for somebody named Ray. What do you think that means?"

"Her husband must have murdered her," I replied.

Two mornings later, Mary Donovan, the night dispatcher at the Bartonsville Police Department, dropped by Tips & Toes for her regularly scheduled nail appointment.

"Heard you visited a psychic the other day," Mary said as she plopped down in front of my nail station.

"How'd you know?"

"Chief Cobb said you called yesterday and demanded that he interview Ray Slocum again because of what the medium told you."

"Dan didn't appear too interested and blew me off."

"He's singing a different tune today," Mary replied. "Patsy's toxicology results came back from the state crime lab this morning."

"And...?"

"It confirmed she was drinking heavily the night of her death, but there were also traces of Rohypnol in her bloodstream."

"Rohypnol? Isn't that a date rape drug?" I asked. "Was Patsy, you know....?"

"Not that we can tell," Mary said. "There wasn't any physical evidence in the hot tub."

"Sounds like Ray's got some explaining to do."

♥ ♥ ♥

As I fumbled to unlock my apartment door that night, I heard my phone ringing in the kitchen.

"Where have you been?" Mandy asked when I picked up the phone. "I've been calling for the past hour."

"I stopped by Grab & Run for a Diet Dr. Pepper. What's up?"

"Have you heard any more about Patsy?"

"Suddenly interested, are you?"

"I was feeling cranky the other day when we met with Madame Filina. I didn't mean to be short with you."

"Apology accepted," I said before telling Mandy what Mary Donovan had told me.

"Why would Ray try to rape Patsy?" Mandy asked. "They were married for Pete sakes."

"You're right, and, besides Ray apparently has an iron clad alibi."

"Huh?"

"Mary said he was in Indy the night that Patsy was found," I said. "But that's not the best part. Remember Judith Rankin?"

"That tall, skinny redhead who was a year behind us in high school?"

"That's her. I ran into her at the Grab & Run. We started talking and I mentioned how Ray had an alibi for Patsy's murder. Judith said she already knew that."

"How?"

"Ray once confessed to her that he and Patsy fooled around on each other."

"Why didn't they get a divorce?"

"Judith says Ray was afraid Patsy's attorney would take him to the cleaners and he'd lose his family's insurance agency."

"So, if Ray has an alibi, what's that malarkey we heard at Madame Filina's?" Mandy asked.

"I wondered that, too, but Judith had a theory. She heard through the grapevine that Patsy loved getting a massage in Indy from some guy named Ramon."

"Hmmm?" Mandy replied. "I guess Ramon sounds a little like Ray."

Tips & Toes is closed on Mondays, so I talked Mandy into driving up to Indianapolis to check out Ramon. It took us about an hour to find his spa in a tiny strip center on the city's southside.

A small sign in the front window read: "Ramon's. His touch will excite your senses."

"Ready to have your senses excited?" I asked.

"Yeah, right," Mandy snorted.

A blonde who looked like she still belonged in high school sat behind a tiny desk in the spa's reception area.

"Do you have an appointment with Ramon?" she asked, letting his name slowly roll off her tongue.

"No, we just need to talk to him about a friend of ours," I replied.

"I'm sorry but Mrs. Richards is already waiting to encounter Ramon," the blonde said, pointing to the frumpy middle-aged woman sitting in the far corner. "When she's finished, perhaps he will grant you a moment."

Mandy and I found a pair of comfortable chairs and some gossip magazines and sat down. A half hour later, a sweaty Mrs. Richards, her suit jacket and purse clutched tightly to her chest, scurried past us and left the spa. Mandy and I turned to each other and began giggling.

"Ramon has granted you five minutes," the blonde interrupted us.

When Mandy and I reached the end of the hallway where we were to encounter Ramon, we noticed instead that the back door was slightly ajar. We opened it wider and spotted a short, slender, dark-haired guy leaning against the brick wall, taking a long drag on a cigarette.

"Are you Ramon?" I asked.

He crushed the cigarette out with his black leather boot and flashed us a wide smile.

"I am Ramon," he replied in a heavy accent. "How can Ramon excite you?"

"Do you know Patsy Slocum?"

"Hmmm?" He rubbed his jaw with his right hand.

"C'mon, Ramon. You remember her," I said. "Tall blonde with a mole on her upper lip and a big set of fake boobies."

"Ah, yes, her," he said, smiling. "But why you ask Ramon this?"

"Guess you haven't heard," I said. "Patsy drowned in her hot tub a few days ago."

"Ramon is sorry to hear this," he said, clearing his throat. "But I don't know why you tell me."

"Cut the crap, Ramon," I said. "We know what you were doing with her."

"Doing with her?" Ramon shook his head as though he didn't understand.

"You know, the mattress mumbo," I said.

"Ramon not understand. I am masseur. Ramon not seduce clients."

I was ready to haul off and whack him when Mandy pulled me back.

"Try something else," she whispered in my ear.

"Ever heard of Bartonsville?" I asked.

"Perhaps," Ramon said cautiously.

"What if I told you we talked to Patsy's neighbors and they told us how they saw the two of you in her hot tub," I said with a straight face.

Ramon's jaw nearly dropped to the ground.

"Okay, you got me," he said, dropping his phony accent. "I once spent the night at Patsy's. Her husband was away on a trip with his golfing buddies. But you must believe me. I didn't kill her. I worshipped the very ground Patsy walked on. I wanted to marry her. But her husband wouldn't give her a divorce."

"Any idea who'd want to kill her?" I asked.

"I don't know," Ramon replied. He suddenly began sobbing uncontrollably and ran back inside the building, slamming the door behind him.

"That was quite an Oscar-winning performance," I said as me and Mandy walked around to the front of the building.

"I don't know," Mandy replied. "I believed him."

♥ ♥ ♥

"Ray did it, didn't he? I knew it."

"No, and neither did Ramon," I said, glaring at Madame Filina an hour later.

"I don't understand," she said with a puzzled look on her face. "Your friend spoke to us. She identified her murderer. Okay, now I get it. Since Ray and this guy you called Ramon didn't do it, you've come here to get your money back, right?"

"No, we're hoping you've got another idea to help us solve Patsy's murder."

"Follow me."

Once we'd sat down at Filina's card table, I asked her point blank. "What's your game plan?"

"We could try contacting your friend like before, but maybe we should try something different," Filina said. "How about Tarot cards?"

"Fine," Mandy replied. "Read Candi's cards."

Thanks, girlfriend.

"Shuffle the deck," Filina said, pushing the giant set of cards towards me.

Filina grabbed the deck when I'd finished and began turning one card over at a time.

"You were married very young, weren't you?"

"Seventeen."

Filina looked at another card.

"But you aren't married anymore."

"Nope. I finally got smart and divorced Bobby's cheating butt."

How can these cards be telling her all that?

"Can you move this along, Filina?" I said, looking at my Betty Boop watch. "We're in a hurry. What else do the cards say?"

"All right, already," she snapped. "Give me a second, will ya?"

Filina stared back down at the cards and suddenly began to frown.

"Something wrong?" I asked.

Filina cleared her throat.

"You'll soon encounter somebody from your past," she said. "But you must be careful. This person may try to harm you."

Early the next morning, I called Mandy on my cell.

"What's up?" she asked.

"Guess who I spotted leaving Ralph's Diner at lunchtime today?"

"I dunno."

"Tony Martucci. Remember him? Or, Trey Thomas as he calls himself today."

"Bartonsville's very own American Idol," Mandy said. "Wonder what he's doing back here?"

"I don't know, but I can't wait to find out."

Two hours later, I called Mandy back.

"Remember how Tony used to have a crush on Patsy in high school? What if he tried to see her again. And what if she blew him off? Besides, don't you think Trey rhymes with Ray? So, maybe we should check him out. What do you think?"

"I think you've been sniffing too much nail polish," Mandy said. "And just how are you going to check him out?"

"I have a plan," I said excitedly.

"Huh?"

"I just called his mother's house and let it slip to him that me and Bobby were divorced and that I hadn't been on a date for a while. Tony took the bait. Asked me to dinner at Ralph's tonight. But that's not all."

"I don't like the sound of that," Mandy said.

"Don't worry," I said. "I told him you and Nate would be joining us."

"Not Nate Sloan."

"Yup, he just left the salon with his mom. She gets her nails done here. Anyway, I told Nate that you'd finally gotten over Melvin's passing and wanted to start dating again. I told him to meet us at the diner at six."

When Tips & Toes closed, I walked a half block to Ralph's Diner. Mandy and Nate were already sitting in the back booth. Nate had a silly grin on his face. And no wonder. This was the closest he'd ever sat to Mandy, his dream girl in high school.

"Where's Tony?" Mandy said.

"He just called me," I said. "He's running late, but he'll be here."

"What's Tony doing back in Bartonsville?" Nate asked.

"He's been back two weeks. Told me his mother is very ill. He's trying to sell her house so he can put her in a nursing home."

As I finished explaining everything to Mandy and Nate, Tony walked through the front door. He still had his dark curly hair and olive complexion and no middle-aged gut like my former Italian stallion, Bobby.

"Hi, everybody," Tony said, sitting down next to me. His cologne was so strong I thought it'd wilt the plastic flower on the table.

"Sorry, we can't stay and have dinner with you kids," Mandy said a few minutes later. "Nate and I have other plans."

What are you doing, Mandy? Leaving me with a potential murderer?

"That's okay," Tony replied. "That'll give me and Candi more time to get re-acquainted. By the way, Nate, congratulations on landing Mandy. She was always a tough nut to crack in high school, if you know what I mean."

I thought Mandy was going to haul off and smack Tony, but she didn't. Instead, she grabbed Nate by the arm, and they left the diner.

Tony moved across to the other side of the booth. I was glad. His cologne was making me nauseous.

"So, how did fatso end up with Mandy?" he asked.

"Mandy says Nate's a terrific lover. The most sensitive man she's ever known."

Tony's remark ticked me off. Nate's no George Clooney. But he's never given me a ticket when he's caught me speeding through town.

"So, how's your singing career coming along?" I asked, changing the subject.

It worked. Tony spent the next twenty minutes explaining how he was singing jingles in LA and got a gig last year aboard a cruise liner. He said the passengers kept calling him the next Frank Sinatra.

"So, what are you doing these days?" he asked me halfway through dinner.

I told Tony how I'd finally saved up enough money to go to cosmetology school and had been working as a manicurist for nearly two years.

"That's nice," he replied, while ordering a slice of coconut crème pie and two forks.

"I'm going to the little girl's room," I said. "When the waitress gets back, tell her I need a refill of my Diet Dr. Pepper."

Once inside a restroom stall, I pulled out my cell phone and called Mandy.

"Why'd you leave me alone with Tony?" I whispered when she picked up.

"I was afraid Tony would find out that Nate's a cop," she replied. "It might have made him suspicious."

"Good point. So where are you now?"

"Nate and I are sitting in my car on the other side of the town square. When you and Tony leave, we'll follow you."

I walked out of the stall, quickly washed my hands and returned to the booth.

"Your refill is here," Tony said as I sat down.

"Thanks."

"Can I tell you a secret?" he asked, leaning across the table and looking directly at me. His eyes were a beautiful slate gray.

"I guess so."

"When we were juniors, I had a serious crush on you."

"You did? So why didn't you talk to me?"

"'Cause I was very shy back then. And by the time I worked up enough courage, Bobby DeCarlo was already dating you. I wasn't going to get in the way of the school's star quarterback."

"That's a sweet story, Tony," I said, taking a big swig of my soft drink.

"I hope you'll let me take you out to dinner again," Tony said. "We could drive up to Indianapolis and go to some fancy place."

"Maybe, but we probably should get going now," I said. "I need to get some rest. We have a busy day at the salon tomorrow."

Once outside, I began to feel woozy and nearly tripped over a crack in the sidewalk.

"Are you okay, Candi?" Tony asked.

"I'm dizzy. Maybe I should sit down for a second."

Tony grabbed my arm and steered me toward his car, which was parked in front of the diner. He helped me into the passenger seat and closed the door.

"Where are we going?" I asked as he backed the car out of the parking space. "You'll see."

Ten minutes later, Tony pulled up in front of a house that looked like his mother's place.

"What are we doing here?" I muttered. I could hardly hold up my head. The last thing I remember was Tony pulling me out of the car and dragging me by the arm toward the house.

Five minutes later, I woke up in a chair long enough to hear someone singing and voices coming through the front door, shouting "Freeze."

♥ ♥ ♥

"Are you okay, sweetie?" Mandy asked when she saw me open my eyes.

"Where am I?"

"Barton Memorial. They brought you here an hour ago."

"Why?"

"Tony must have slipped some Rohypnol into your drink at the diner and drove you to his mother's house."

"Were you there, too?"

"Yep, don't you remember? Nate and I followed you from the diner. He called for reinforcements when Tony dragged you inside the house."

"Wow," I said, trying to sit up in bed. "He didn't, you know, did he?"

"Nope. He was sitting across from you in the living room singing you a love ballad."

"That's different."

"You're right," Mandy said.

"Where's Nate?"

"He and the other cops took Tony into custody. I suspect they'll get him to confess to Patsy's murder before the night is over."

"Why would Tony want to kill Patsy?" I asked.

"Probably because she didn't want to be bothered with him," Mandy replied. "You know how some guys can't stand rejection."

"Damn him," I said. "I hope Tony gets what's coming to him."

"I'm sure he will," Mandy said. "But, where are you going now?"

I had swung my legs over the side of the bed and was preparing to jump down.

"I need to call Madame Filina," I said.

"What for?"

"Don't you remember? She told me I'd meet somebody from my past and he'd try to harm me."

"So?"

"If she can do that, maybe she can tell me when I'm going to meet a tall, dark and handsome stranger."

Originally published in the Strange Mysteries 2 Anthology, *Whortleberry Press, 2009.*

That Ugly Painting

"**W**here'd you get that ugly painting?" Mandy Malone, my best friend since kindergarten, shouted from the middle of my tiny living room on Sunday morning.

"At an estate sale last Friday while on my way to work," I said, stepping out of my bathroom. "Do you like it?"

"No, it's ugly."

"No, it's not."

"Yes, it is. How much did you pay for it?"

"Twenty dollars" I said. "It's an abstract. It's supposed to be unusual. I think it looks great." I eyed it hanging there on the wall between my two small windows.

"You were robbed," Mandy said, turning away from the painting. "Wait a minute, you're not wearing that outfit to go shopping, are you?"

"Huh?" I said, glancing down at my black miniskirt to see if Mandy had spotted a stain. "What's wrong with it?"

"Candi DeCarlo, you're over forty. Women our age don't dress like that when shopping at the Fashion Mall," Mandy said. She was wearing a beige silk blouse and floral print skirt that reached down to her ankles. "You might wear that if you're looking to get lucky on Saturday night at Rick's Hideaway Lounge, but not to go shopping in Indianapolis. Put on a pair of slacks instead."

"Whatever," I sighed before turning on my four-inch heels and stomping off to my bedroom. "When did you become my mother?" I muttered under my breath.

It was nearing six o'clock when Mandy dropped me off in front of my duplex on Elm Street and sped away in her shiny, black Jaguar.

I trudged up the rickety outside steps that led to my second-floor apartment. It'd been a productive shopping trip. Lots of fifty percent off sales. My hands were full of shopping bags.

Once on the landing, I dropped the bags and rummaged through my hobo bag looking for my keys. As I stuck the key into the lock, I noticed one of the panes of glass in my front door was busted. I twisted the doorknob and the door opened in my hand. Damn. Somebody'd broken into my apartment! I dug through my bag for my pepper spray. Somebody was about to become a blind man.

"Anybody here?" I shouted as I stepped through the front door.

That was dumb, Candi. Nothing like letting the burglar know you're home.

Fortunately, nobody answered. I headed straight for my bedroom to see if the burglar had taken any of my clothes or costume jewelry, but nothing appeared to be missing.

When I stepped back into the living room, I noticed my new abstract painting was missing. Snatched right off the wall. Who'd stolen it? I reached for the cell phone in my bag and called Mandy.

"Somebody broke into my apartment while we were shopping and took my new painting," I yelled into the phone after she picked up.

"Who knew Bartonsville still had a good Samaritan?"

"That's not funny, Mandy," I said. "I really love that painting. What should I do?"

I suppose you could offer a thousand-dollar reward for its safe return, or file a missing painting report with the police."

It was just after three on Tuesday afternoon when Mary Donovan, a dispatcher with the Bartonsville Police Department, walked into Tips & Toes for her regular nail appointment.

"Heard your place was burglarized the other night," she said, plopping down in front of my nail station.

"Yeah they stole my new painting right off the wall," I replied.

"I also heard you bought it last week at Agnes Murphy's estate sale."

"Yup. So, have you guys found it yet?"

"No, but I talked to Chief Cobb briefly before coming over here," Mary said. "Your case is more complicated than he first thought."

"What do you mean?"

"The Chief's first homicide when he worked for the Indianapolis Metropolitan Police Department involved a reclusive art collector named Russell Thompson. The Chief and his fellow detectives believed two men broke into Thompson's house on North Meridian Street a dozen years ago, stabbed him to death and made off with his most valuable paintings."

"Did they ever find the murderers?" I asked.

"No. It's a cold case, but the Chief says he always had a gut feeling about who did it."

"I don't understand. What's that got to do with my missing painting?"

"Among the suspects were two guys from the Bartonsville area, but IMPD couldn't prove they stabbed Thompson."

"Wow," I said. "Does the Chief also think those guys stole my painting?"

"I can't say anything more," Mary said. "I've already told you too much. Let's try a different color on my nails today."

After Mary left with her new tangerine nails, I started thinking about the two Bartonsville guys she mentioned that were art thieves and murderers. Who were they? I must have known them. I knew practically everyone in town. And finally, were they the ones that broke into my apartment and stole my abstract painting? I needed some answers and fast. I missed my painting.

I called Mandy to ask her for some advice. "What are you doing?" I asked when she picked up.

"Ravishing the boy toy who showed up on my doorstep a half hour ago," she replied. "What do you think I'm doing?"

"Let's see, its eight o'clock," I said, after glancing at my Betty Boop watch. "You're probably taking a bubble bath and sipping a glass of champagne."

"Bingo. You win. Why are you calling me? You know I hate being disturbed while I'm enjoying my bubbles."

I apologized and then told Mandy what Mary Donovan had said about the two Bartonsville guys suspected of murdering an Indianapolis art collector and how they may have stolen my painting.

"That's highly unlikely," Mandy said when I finished. "Why would two guys who are used to stealing valuable paintings want your ugly thing?"

Mandy had a point. I only paid twenty dollars for my painting, but it wasn't ugly like she kept claiming. It held a lot of sentimental value. It's the first time I've bought a painting somewhere other than Walmart.

"Remind me again where you bought that ugly painting?" Mandy said.

"At Agnes Murphy's estate sale."

"I remember her. Sweet old lady, but she had this worthless nephew named Peter Shaw. He hung out in the same motorcycle gang with my first husband, Butch Muldoon. They called him Dead Eye Pete because he wore a black patch over his left eye and he could shoot a gun really well."

"Sounds charming," I said. "Did Dead Eye have any close friends?"

"Yeah, a cousin," Mandy said. "Weird Willy Watson. Sounds like a professional wrestler, doesn't he? The story goes that Willy earned his nickname for doing crazy things when he drank too much or smoked pot."

"Think they still live in Bartonsville?"

"Doubt it," Mandy replied. "Last I heard Dead Eye and my ex-husband were cellmates at Pendleton. Each doing ten years for beating up a liquor store clerk one night. I don't know about Willy. Why?"

"I want to ask him if he stole my painting."

"Candi, you're crazy. Even if you find Willy, he's not going to admit to stealing your ugly painting. Instead, he's liable to hurt you for asking. Stay away from him."

I decided to ignore Mandy's advice. Despite her warning, I needed to check out Weird Willy on my own, so after work on Wednesday night, I came home, changed into my shortest miniskirt and tightest sweater I could find in my closet, and drove to Rick's Hideaway Lounge. I figured Willy might hang out there.

"Well, look who's here," Rick Ives said as I strutted into his bar. "You're looking mighty fine tonight, Candi. What brings you out on a weeknight? Can I get you a drink?"

"I'm looking for a guy," I said as I sat down on a barstool and waited on Rick to fix me a strawberry daiquiri. "Weird Willy Watson."

"What do you want with that troublemaker?" Rick asked, setting the daiquiri down in front of me.

"I need to ask him a few questions," I said, sipping my drink. It tasted wonderful.

Before Rick could reply, someone spun me around on my barstool and planted a juicy, wet kiss on my lips. It was my ex-husband Bobby DeCarlo. Damn, he still looked as good as he did back in high school.

"What are you doin' here, Candi?" he asked, wiping pink lipstick off his lips. "Still looking for the man of your dreams?"

"No. I don't need another guy to ruin my life," I said. "I was asking Rick if he knew Wild Willy Watson."

"I know that dude," Bobby said, sitting down next to me. "We've worked on a couple construction jobs. He's a decent carpenter. Saw him last week outside the courthouse. Wondered if he was in trouble with the law again."

"Know where he lives?"

"Wait a minute, Candi, you're not thinking of hooking up with him, are you?" Bobby asked. "Willy's bad news."

"No, I only want to talk to him."

"Yeah, I know where Willy lives, but it's going to cost you."

"You're not getting another kiss," I said. "Rick, grab Bobby a beer, and put it on my tab."

"You don't need to buy me a beer," Bobby said, as he grabbed the bottle from Rick. "I was hoping you'd like to do something else tonight if you catch my drift."

"Bobby, I'm not interested in you anymore," I said. "Remember, we're divorced."

"I know…I know," he said, taking another long swig of his beer. "Remind me again how all that happened."

"Simple. You liked spending more time with your girl-friends than you did with me. Now, are you going to give me Willy's address?"

I took a pen out of my bag and reached across the bar for a paper napkin so Bobby could write down directions. When he finished, I slapped a ten on the bar and shouted to Rick, "Bring Bobby another beer, and keep the change."

"Thanks, Candi," Bobby said as he slammed his empty beer bottle on the bar.

Once outside, I glanced at my watch. It was nearing nine o'clock. Probably too late to pay a visit to Willy's house. Besides,

I had a busy schedule tomorrow at Tips & Toes and needed to go home and get some beauty rest.

Thursday turned out to be a bust at work. A couple clients called early to cancel their afternoon appointments. I hate it when that happens. It means fewer tips in my pocket.

I hurried home from work, ate a small salad from the Grab & Run, and then stood in front of my clothes closet trying to decide what to wear to Willy's place. How about an outfit like I wore last night to Rick's Hideaway? No, Willy might get the wrong idea about my visit. I settled for black jeans and a loose-fitting top.

Willy lived at the Shady Pines Trailer Park on the east side of town. I knew the place very well. My mother, my half-brother, and I lived there for a short time while I was growing up. It's now a dump. I steered my F-150 down the main gravel road. Willy's mobile home was next to a bright yellow trailer with at least a dozen wind chimes, just like Bobby had drawn on his map. After parking out front, I walked up to his front door and knocked.

"Come on in, the doors open," I heard a voice calling from somewhere inside the trailer.

I stepped through the doorway. Willy was sitting in a broken-down faux leather recliner in the middle of his living room. He wasn't anything like I imagined. Willy had to lose weight to get to three hundred pounds. He was wearing a dirty white T-shirt and wrinkled black pants, and he had big holes in his smelly-looking athletic socks.

"Well, well," Willy said, a big smile forming on his face. "Who are you, darling?"

I was ready for his question. On my way to his place, I made up a story about why I was there.

"I'm Candi. Your landlord hired me to find out what he can do to make the trailer park a better place to live."

"Looking to raise my rent again, is he?" Willy said. "How much time you got to listen to my complaints?"

"A few minutes," I said, pulling a small notebook and pen out of my bag. "Go ahead whenever you are ready."

Willy was like the Hoover dam suddenly bursting at its seams. He spent the next fifteen minutes talking non-stop about everything that was wrong with the trailer park. It included the unpaved roads, potholes as big as moon craters, and weeds growing alongside the road as high as some of the trailers. I didn't expect a guy like Willy to even notice his surroundings.

I sat across from him on the edge of his couch and pretended to write down his every word. Actually, I scribbled circles in my notebook while casually glancing around the living room for any sign of my painting or any other artwork he'd stolen.

Willy had moved on to the trailer park's faulty septic system when the front door opened and in walked a tall, heavy-set woman with a cigarette dangling from her lips.

"What's going on here?" she screamed after spotting me. "Who's this bimbo, Willy? One of your little girlfriends?"

"No, Melissa, Candi's doing a survey for our landlord," Willy tried to explain, but his friend wasn't in any mood to listen.

She hovered over me like a linebacker glaring down at a quarterback he'd just sacked. "If I were you, missy," she said in a deep voice, "I'd get the hell out of here now while you're still in one piece."

Melissa didn't have to tell me twice. I jumped off the couch and was out the door in a flash. As I made my way back to my truck, I could hear Willy and Melissa yelling at each other inside their trailer.

Love was sure complicated at times.

Before going to work on Friday morning, I dropped by Ralph's Diner for my usual — a cinnamon swirl and Diet Dr. Pepper. I'd just taken the first bite of the swirl when I heard my name.

I turned around on the lunch counter stool. Chief Dan Cobb was standing beside me. I swear, he's the best-looking single man in Bartonsville.

"Hi, Chief," I said while trying to swallow the doughy swirl stuffed in my mouth. "What brings you here this morning?"

"Looking for you," he replied as he sat down on the stool next to me.

Oh my God, Dan's finally going to ask me out!

"Were you at William Watson's place last night?

I grabbed my Diet Dr. Pepper and took a long swig.

How'd he know that?

"I'm waiting, Candi," the Chief said, tapping his fingers on the lunch counter.

"Yeah, I may have been there. You know, I used to live in that trailer park."

"You went there to see if Watson stole your painting, didn't you?"

"Maybe," I finally replied. I hate it when Chief Cobb grills me like a common criminal.

"I know because Mary told me all about her conversation with you the other day. I don't know how you learned Watson's name, but when my officers arrived at his place last night to break up the domestic dispute, Watson's girlfriend, Melissa Sharp, said the fight began over some girl named Candi. And, you're the only Candi I know in Bartonsville."

Darn, I should have used a fake name to go along with my fake story.

"So," I said, taking another sip of my Dr. Pepper.

"So, I don't want you investigating burglaries on your own. Watson is a dangerous guy and so is his girlfriend. She tried to bite one of my officers. Besides, you may have tipped him off about being a suspect in your burglary and possibly that cold case murder that Mary mentioned.

"Sorry, Dan. I didn't mean to do anything wrong. I simply want my painting back."

"Visiting Watson's place wasn't the right way to go about it. Do you understand?"

"I said I was sorry."

"So, did you talk to Watson while you were inside his trailer?"

"Yes," I replied. "I pretended to be taking a survey about repairs needed at the trailer park."

"Did you see anything unusual while you were there?"

Wait a minute. Dan's wanting me to be a snitch for him. So now it's okay that I went there.

"Nothing at first, but before I left, I noticed an empty picture frame propped against the wall next to Watson's recliner," I said. "But it wasn't mine, so I didn't accuse him of anything. I wanted to get out of there before his girlfriend broke me in two."

"That's interesting," Chief Cobb said. "I'll get back to you."

My boss, Madge Parsons, leaned down beside me on Saturday afternoon as I was applying a set of acrylic nails for my eighty-year-old client, Lonnie Sparks. "A strange-looking woman up front wants to speak with you right away," Madge whispered in my ear.

I looked up and spotted Weird Willy Watson's girlfriend, Melissa.

What's she doing here?

I asked Lonnie if she could wait a few minutes. She was in no hurry.

As Madge and I walked towards the front, I asked her to stand next to the phone and call 9-1-1 if Melissa followed through on her earlier promise to break me into pieces.

"What can I do for you, Melissa?" I asked.

"We need to talk. Alone."

"The laundry room," I said, pointing to the rear of the salon.

Once in the room, Melissa insisted that I close the door. I was reluctant at first, but since she'd asked in such a calm voice, I figured she wasn't planning to hit me right away.

"I need to clear up a few things with you," she said.

"If this is about Willy, I'm not one of his girlfriends."

"No kidding," she said. "You're not his type. He likes big, full-bodied women like me. Not skinny babes like you."

"I wasn't sure how to react to Melissa's comment. I'm a hot babe.

"What were you really doing at our place?" Melissa asked.

"My neighbor said you didn't stop by her place with any survey. She also knows you work here. Tell me the truth. Why were you talking with Willy?"

I looked at Melissa and could tell she was being sincere, so I told her how I suspected that Willy broke into my apartment on Sunday afternoon and stole my favorite abstract painting. I tried saying it as nicely as I could so she wouldn't go ballistic. She didn't.

"Funny you mentioned that," Melissa said. "Willy's been acting strange lately."

"How so?"

"He got a call from his cousin, Peter Shaw. Willy told me later that they talked about some artwork. Then, Willy went to check on some paintings at this old woman's estate sale. He never goes to auctions."

"Melissa, I think Willy and Peter murdered an Indianapolis art collector a decade ago and stole some of his valuable paintings. They must have hidden them at Agnes's house."

Melissa looked stunned. Then she turned and stormed out of the laundry room. "Wait till I get my hands on Willy," she shouted.

"Stop Melissa," I yelled at her, but she was already at the front door. Confronting Willy on her own didn't sound like a good idea to me. I went back to my nail station to finish Lonnie's acrylic nails. Then, I called the Police Department and asked for Mary Donovan. I told her of Melissa's visit.

"I'll have Chief Cobb check out Watson's place," Mary said. "I agree. It sounds like his girlfriend could be in danger."

After hanging up, I glanced at the clock on the back wall. It was nearing four o'clock. I tidied up my station before telling Madge I needed to leave early to run an errand.

As I drove up to Willy Watson's trailer fifteen minutes later, I noticed three police cars parked out front with their red lights blazing.

I stepped out of my truck and walked towards Watson's trailer. "What's going on?" I asked a neighbor who was standing there.

"I think the cops are going to arrest Willy," the woman replied. "If you ask me. It's about time they nailed him for all the terrible things he's done to Melissa in the past."

A few minutes later, two officers walked out of Willy's trailer carrying several paintings. They opened the trunk of their cruiser and carefully placed them inside. A third officer brought out Willy in handcuffs and not-so-carefully placed him in the backseat of his cruiser. Finally, Chief Cobb and Melissa appeared. The Chief said something to her before speeding away in his own car.

All this time I stood behind the woman I'd been talking to so Chief Cobb wouldn't see me and yell at me for being there.

Once the cops left, I walked up to Melissa. She was still standing in front of her trailer with her arms crossed.

"What happened, Melissa?" I asked.

"You were right, Candi," she said. "Willy and his cousin did steal some paintings a long time ago. He also admitted to breaking into your apartment."

"Did he tell you why?"

"He didn't get the chance," Melissa said. "The cops pulled up right then and arrested him."

"Did you happen to see my painting?"

♥ ♥ ♥

On Sunday afternoon, I was watching a made-for-TV movie on the Hallmark Channel when my doorbell rang. It was Chief Cobb.

"What are you doing here?" I asked after opening the front door.

"I've got something for you," he said, reaching behind his back and pulling out my abstract painting.

"It's still part of our evidence," he explained. "After stealing the collector's paintings, Willy and his cousin realized reputable collectors weren't interested in buying stolen property, so they hired a neighborhood kid to paint some blank canvasses. They placed them in front of the collector's originals and hid them at Agnes Murphy's place. When she passed away, Willy tried to retrieve them at her estate sale, but he apparently missed the one you bought."

"Thanks for returning it," I said, hugging my painting. All I needed now was to buy a new picture frame at Walmart.

Originally published in the Fine Art of Murder Anthology, *Blue River Press, 2016.*

Candy Bags

Let me offer you some friendly advice: never get on my friend, Mandy Malone's bad side.

Believe me, I know what I'm talking about. Last weekend, I thought my friendship with my life-long bestie had come to an end.

It all started last Monday when Martha Rae Folger, general manager of WYMN-AM, our town's radio station, stopped by Tips & Toes. As I applied some bright red polish to her nails, Martha Rae told me about the Halloween party that the radio station and the Bartonsville Middle School Parent-Teacher Organization was planning on Saturday night.

"It will be held in the school gym, so the kiddos don't have to trek door-to-door if it rains or snows. It also eliminates the chance of a kid ending up with an unsafe treat, thanks to one of our Neanderthal neighbors."

"What a terrific idea," I replied. "Kids need to be kept safe from the town's sickos. What can I do to help?"

"I'm still looking for event sponsors. Think Madge might help us?"

Madge Parsons owns Tips & Toes. She's not terribly civ-ic-minded and complains every year when she has to pay her share for the July 4th fireworks display the merchants hold on the town square.

"Doubt it," I said. "Madge doesn't like parting with her money unless she's standing in front of a slot machine at a riverboat casino along the Ohio River."

"What about your friend, Mandy Malone?" Martha Rae asked. "Think she'd help? She inherited a successful chain of discount tire stores in southern Indiana when her husband died."

"Mandy is like Madge. She likes to spend her money on herself. And, she really isn't into kids except for my daughter, Jenny, her goddaughter, and Jenny's two kids. She loves to show up with toys for Jacob and Abby when they visit me."

"Candi, you can be persuasive," Martha Rae said. "Get Mandy to help us out."

That night, I called Mandy, but not until after eight-thirty. She takes a nightly bubble bath and hates being disrupted during her nightly ritual.

"What's up?" Mandy asked after picking up her phone.

"Not much," I said. "It was pretty boring at the salon today. Except, I had an interesting conversation with Martha Rae Folger."

"What's going on with the town's leading gossip?"

No doubt, Mandy was thinking of Martha Rae's afternoon talk show where listeners call in and talk about anything on their minds. Sometimes, the conversations get out of hand. And when that happens, the person under attack usually complains that the show is an example of fake news.

"The radio station and middle school PTO are having a Halloween party for the kids on Saturday night." I said.

"Why should I care about that?"

"Martha Rae wants you to contribute to the party."

"Why would I do that?" Mandy said. "I hate kids."

"I know," I replied. "But this could be good for your business."

"How?" Mandy said. "Kids don't buy tires."

"But their parents do. And, they'll appreciate that you were an event sponsor. Besides, Martha Rae said she'll feature each sponsor on her show before Saturday's party."

"Hmmm?" Mandy replied. "Maybe I could write her a check. Find out how much she needs."

The next day, Mandy wrote a $250 check for the party. The money would help pay for the candy and juice boxes. Martha Rae kept her promise. She invited Mandy to appear on her show at least three times.

I could tell Mandy enjoyed the free publicity, but it was a conversation that we had during one of our nightly calls that surprised me.

"Martha Rae wants me to wear a costume to the party," she said.

"What did you tell her?"

"I'd only do it if you came along."

"Why me?"

"I don't want to go there by myself and be surrounded by a bunch of screaming kids."

"So, what kind of costume do you plan to wear?" I asked.

"I don't know yet," Mandy replied. "That's why I'm hanging up so I can check out the possibilities on the internet."

It was a little after six on Saturday night when I heard a car horn blaring on the street below. It had to be Mandy. She hates climbing the outside stairs to my second-floor apartment. She says it makes her sweat and messes up her makeup.

I picked up my jacket and ran downstairs and jumped into her black Jaguar convertible.

"Ready to party?" Mandy asked as we sped away from the curb.

"What are you wearing?" I said after turning and staring at her.

"I'm Wonder Woman."

"Where'd you get your costume?"

"I found one on the internet, but I was afraid it wouldn't arrive in time. So, I found a costume shop in Indianapolis. It cost me fifty bucks to rent it, plus a fifty-dollar deposit in case I don't return it."

"Isn't it a little provocative for a kid's party?"

"What do you mean?" Mandy asked.

"Oh, I don't know. Maybe it's the red bustier and blue and white polka-dot hot pants. And those knee-high red stockings with the black garter belt. Where did you get them?"

"The costume place didn't have any stockings, so I bought these at a sexy lingerie shop nearby. Who are you pretending to be?"

"Dolly Parton."

"Figures. Where'd you get that silver sequined dress with its plunging neckline? I don't recall ever seeing it in your closet."

"It wasn't there until Wednesday night when I stopped by the Goodwill store after work and found this little beauty on a rack in the far corner of the store."

"Aren't you afraid your girls might fall out?"

"Naw, they'll be safe," I said. "I'm wearing a brand-new bra."

"And, the long blonde hair?"

"It's a wig. It belonged to my mom. I didn't have time after work to curl my own hair, so I'm wearing the wig instead."

"Aren't we a pair," Mandy said.

Martha Rae Folger, dressed as the good witch Glinda from *The Wizard of Oz*, greeted us at the entrance to the middle school gym.

"What do you need us to do?" I asked.

"Nothing. The PTO has created a carnival-like atmosphere inside with lots of games and prizes for the kids," she said. "Just float around and talk to them and their parents. You girls look ravaging. Are you going to an adult party after this one?"

"No, we don't have any plans," Mandy said.

Martha Rae excused herself to greet other arriving sponsors. As Mandy and I began walking around the outer edge of the gym, we soon noticed that we were being followed. At least a half dozen pre-teens and a couple of dads, their mouths hanging open, saddled up to us and offered to run and get us juice boxes if we were thirsty.

Mandy turned to me and with a giant smile said, "We still got it, girlfriend."

We giggled and gave each other a high-five.

A minute later, a heart-piercing shriek came from the middle of the gym floor. It brought the place to a standstill.

"What was that?" Mandy asked.

"Sounds like something bad has happened."

As Mandy and I moved closer, we spotted a boy sprawled on the floor. A woman was leaning next to him, trying to keep his head up and shouting for someone to call for an ambulance.

"What happened?" I asked a woman standing next to me.

"The boy must suffer from food allergies," the woman replied. "My son does, too. He must have eaten some bad candy."

Within five minutes, paramedics had arrived. They quickly placed the boy on a stretcher and whisked him off to the Bartonsville Memorial Hospital emergency room. Soon after they left, the party broke up. Parents grabbed their kid's bags of candy and threw them in garbage receptacles as they stormed out of the gym.

I glanced around for Mandy, but didn't see her anywhere. I asked the woman still standing next to me if she had seen her.

"You mean that hussy dressed as Wonder Woman?" the woman replied. "She should be ashamed of herself for arousing impure thoughts among several hormone-crazed boys."

"That hussy happens to be my best friend," I said. "Do you know where she went?"

"Yeah, I saw her leave the gym. She was yelling hysterically about not wanting to be sued."

It was a little after ten o'clock on Sunday morning when my phone rang. I was enjoying some toast and coffee at my kitchen table. Mandy's calling to apologize for stranding me at the gym and forcing me to hitch a ride home with a neighbor.

The caller was Martha Rae Folger.

"Have you heard from Mandy this morning?" she asked.

"I tried calling her a few times, but she didn't answer. She's either ignoring me, or she drove to Indy to return her Wonder Woman outfit. It had to be back today, or she'd lose her fifty-dollar costume deposit."

"Any idea why Mandy left the gym so abruptly last night?"

"Not really," I said. "But a woman next to me thought she heard Mandy shouting something about being sued."

"Why would she say that?" Martha Rae asked.

"I have an idea," I replied. "Two weeks ago, Mandy attended a business conference in Indy. One of the speakers talked about how plaintiff attorneys are really vultures who love to sue businesses when some alleged harm comes to a customer. Maybe, Mandy was worried the boy's parents might sue the party sponsors."

"Mandy's instincts weren't too far off," Martha Rae said. "*The Barton County Beacon* published a brief story this morning in which the boy's parents said they intend to sue the radio station, the PTO and anybody else if anything bad happens to their son."

"Oh, great," I said. "Heard anything more about the kid's condition?"

"My reporter, Johnny Edwards, just checked with hospital officials. They confirmed the boy did suffer from a food allergy. He's still in the intensive care unit, but they said he'll be okay."

"That's great news," I said. "Any idea how he ended up eating the wrong candy?"

"Good question," Martha Rae replied. "The PTO was adamant that we offer kids two types of candy bags. One with nutty candy and one without. Unfortunately, the PTO couldn't find enough volunteers to bag the bulk candy we bought so the residents at the Springs of Bartonsville offered to help."

"Listen, I know Margaret Sullivan, the facility's administrator," I said. "Let me see if she knows what happened."

It was a little after two o'clock when I parked my Ford F-150 in front of the main entrance to the Springs, the town's newest assisted-living facility. I had called ahead to make sure Margaret Sullivan would be there.

She greeted me at the front door before we walked back to her office.

"What can I do for you today, Candi?" Margaret asked.

I quickly described what happened Saturday night at the school gym and asked if she knew how a candy bag could have been contaminated with nuts.

"That's interesting," Margaret said when I finished. "My PTO contact called me at home an hour ago. She was frantic. She also told me about last night and the article in today's paper. The boy's parents want to sue everyone, including us. That's why I came into work right away to get to the bottom of this matter."

"Are you any closer to solving the mystery of what happened?" I asked.

"Not yet," Margaret said. "Projects like stuffing candy bags help keep our residents' minds active. It is a good alternative to them simply watching TV or playing bingo all day. We set up two tables, one for candy having nuts and one without. Obviously, a nutty candy bag ended up in the wrong pile."

"How could that have happened," I asked.

"I'm not sure, but I know who to ask," Margaret said as she stood up and headed for her office door.

"Where are we going?"

"To visit Agnes McDonald," Margaret replied. "She supervised the non-nut table."

It took us five minutes to walk to Agnes McDonald's one-bedroom apartment at the far end of the facility.

"Margaret, what a delightful surprise," Agnes said after opening her front door and inviting us into her living room. "And, who is this lovely lady with you?"

"This is Candi DeCarlo," Margaret replied. "We're here to ask you some questions about the candy bag project."

"Oh, yes, it was such a wonderful experience to help the kids celebrate Halloween safely," Agnes said, before adding, "But, I must be honest. It was also a bit tedious. We had to stick the same amount of candy in each bag all afternoon."

"You must like sweets, Agnes," I said, noticing a bowl full of candy on her coffee table. "Mind if I have one?"

"Help yourself, dear," she said. "I'm glad someone else has a sweet tooth, too."

I grabbed one of the candies, unpeeled its silver wrapper, and popped it in my mouth.

"This is delicious," I said between chews. "What are they called?"

"Chocolate hazelnut balls," Agnes said. "They're my favorite."

"Were they part of the candy bag project?" Margaret asked.

"Yes, but they were on the other table." Agnes replied.

"Are you sure a few didn't end up on your table by mistake?" I asked.

Agnes dropped her head slightly.

"I had a few sitting next to me, but I swear none of them ended up in my bags. I needed them for energy while we spent the afternoon filling the bags."

"I understand, but is it possible someone else dropped them in a bag?" I asked.

"It's possible," Agnes said. "I did step away from the table at the end of the day to count the filled bags we had placed on another table. Perhaps one of my helpers shoved them into a bag. We were trying to finish quickly because it was time for dinner."

Margaret and I thanked Agnes for her time and left her apartment.

"Mystery solved?" Margaret asked as we walked back to the main entrance.

"I think so," I replied.

Once outside the Springs of Bartonsville, I called Martha Rae Folger to tell her my news.

"That's terrific," she said when I finished. "I also have some good news. I just spoke to a hospital official. The boy has fully recovered and will be released later today."

I thanked Martha Rae and told her that I needed to hang up so I could call Mandy.

She answered her phone after three rings.

"Where have you been?" I asked.

"I just drove back from Indy," Mandy replied. "I had to return my Wonder Woman costume. I didn't want to lose my deposit."

"Why didn't you answer your phone when I called this morning?"

"I was still mad at you."

"Why?"

"It was all your idea to involve me in that damn kid's party. After that kid fell on the floor, I figured I'd be sued and lose my business. Marvin would rollover in his grave and my stepson would blame me for ruining his inheritance."

"Calm down," I said. "Martha Rae says the kid is okay and he'll soon leave the hospital. I also learned where the bad candy came from."

"What?"

"One of the ladies at the Springs of Bartonsville accidentally tossed it in the wrong bag."

"So, it's not my fault?"

"No, and I suspect that once the boy's parents learn what happened, they'll forget about suing anyone."

"Candi, you're my savior," Mandy said. "How can I repay you?"

"Buy me a bag of chocolate hazelnut balls."

Murder in the Corn Maze

Carolyn Tinsdale has been the news and farm director at WYMN-AM in Bartonsville, Indiana, for nearly twenty years and seldom has missed a day of work. That's why I was surprised when Patty Black, our new morning-on-air personality, called me just after six on Tuesday to say Caroline hadn't shown up for work.

"Did you call her house?" I asked, trying to rub the sleep dust from my eyes.

"Yup, but there was no answer."

I hung up on Patty and scrambled out of bed. Where was Caroline? It wasn't like her to miss work and not call, but I didn't have time to worry about it right now. WYMN-AM needed to be on the air at sunrise. I quickly showered and threw on some clothes before heading out the front door. Once at the station, I pulled together the opening corn and livestock market prices, grabbed a handful of stories off the news wire and handled Caroline's seven and eight o'clock newscasts. When I finished, I made a beeline for my tiny, windowless office where

I finally enjoyed a second cup of coffee when my private line rang. It was Caroline.

"Where are you?" I asked.

"At the county jail. Sheriff Pickle's taken Frank into custody."

"Why?"

"Frank found Malcolm McGregor in the middle of our corn maze early this morning. He was shot twice in the back."

"I'll be right there."

The Barton County sheriff's department and adjoining jail complex sits on the western edge of town. It took me ten minutes to drive over there. After parking my yellow Beetle out front, I entered the two-story brick building and found Carolyn curled up on a plastic chair in the corner of the lobby.

"Where's Frank?"

"They're still questioning him."

"Tell me again what happened?"

"Some unruly teenagers came through the maze last night, and Frank was worried they might have toppled some corn stocks. So, he left the house before sunrise to check on everything. That's when he found Malcolm lying face down in a clearing. He had two bullet holes in his back.

"I'm sorry, but I still don't understand. Why's the sheriff questioning Frank? He didn't shoot Malcolm, did he?"

"Of course not, but after the sheriff took Frank's statement, we were walking back to the house when a deputy ran up to us and said he'd just found Frank's shotgun in the barn. It had been recently fired."

"That's outrageous," I said. "Melvin Pickle knows perfectly well that Frank wouldn't harm a flea, much less shoot Malcolm. It's time to get to the bottom of this."

I stood up and marched over to the front counter where a pudgy, middle-aged deputy was leafing through a fishing magazine.

"I need to speak with the sheriff right away."

The deputy slowly looked up from his magazine and asked for my name.

"I'm Martha Rae Folger, general manager of WYMN-AM. Tell Pickle I'm here about Malcolm McGregor's murder."

The deputy picked up his phone and mumbled something into the receiver. A few minutes later, Sheriff Melvin T. Pickle came waltzing into the lobby.

To say Melvin's short would be an understatement. I'm five feet four inches in my stocking feet, and he barely comes up to my shoulders. Melvin's been sheriff for nearly thirty years and has developed his favorites during that time, but I'm not one of them.

"Well, well, well…what brings the town's media darling to my humble office this morning?" Melvin asked.

I really wanted to punch him in the gut, but thought better of it. I didn't have time to get locked up today.

"Why are you still questioning Frank Tinsdale?" I asked, flashing him my best glare. "You know darn well he couldn't have murdered Malcolm McGregor."

"I'm afraid the evidence is pretty overwhelming," Melvin said, scratching his buzz cut. "But it ain't my call. I'm meeting the prosecutor this afternoon. Until then, Frank's staying put. And, that's all I'm saying."

With that, Melvin turned and abruptly walked away. Damn him. He didn't even say good-bye.

Carolyn ran up to my side. "What did Melvin say?"

"I think you need to find a good lawyer, sweetie."

My afternoon talk show, "Over the Back Fence," follows the two o'clock news. Folks can call in and say whatever's on their minds. Sometimes, the show can get pretty lively, especially if someone is mad with a neighbor and wants everyone else in town to know about it. That could be why Sheriff Pickle doesn't like me. His deputies probably have broken up a few of those neighborly disputes.

For some reason, the phone lines were unusually quiet so I launched into a monologue on why Frank Tinsdale couldn't have murdered Malcolm McGregor. When I finished, the lines on my radio console lit up like a Christmas tree.

"If Frank murdered Malcolm, then I'm a mass murderer," one elderly woman said. Other callers offered similar sentiments. Nobody, it seems, believed that Frank shot Malcolm.

They'd been neighbors and best friends for years. And, besides, why would Frank kill Malcolm just before Halloween? Frank and Carolyn owned the only corn maze in Barton County and made enough money from letting folks traipse through it each October to keep their farm operating the rest of the year.

When my show ended at five o'clock, I put on some pre-recorded music before leaving the main studio. The music would play until the station went off the air at 6:15 p.m. As I stepped into my office. I heard my private line ringing.

"Carolyn," I said, picking up the receiver. "Is that you?"

"No, it's Johnny Edwards."

"How'd you get this number?"

"I have my ways."

Indeed, Johnny seemed to have his ways, not all of which I completely understood. He'd been a star football and basketball player at Bartonsville High School in the early nineties before he'd run off to join the Marines. A year later, he came home from Desert Storm with one less leg and some missing fingers after stepping on a roadside bomb. Now, Johnny spends his days tooling around town in a motorized wheelchair, putting himself in the middle of everyone else's business.

"What can I do for you, Johnny?"

"Heard your show this afternoon?"

"And..."

Something told me that wasn't why he was calling.

"And, you've got it all wrong about Frank Tinsdale."

"What do you mean?"

"Frank and Malcolm got into a shouting match at the zoning board meeting last week. Malcolm and his brother want to rezone their farm and sell it. Frank said they'd have to do it over his dead body."

I wanted to remind Johnny that it wasn't Frank who was now dead, but I got his point.

"That so," I finally replied. "But that doesn't prove anything."

"Maybe , but enough people heard Frank's comment that it could come back to haunt him if he goes on trial."

Damn. Johnny was right. Something like that could hurt Frank's case. I was tired and not up to a lengthy repartee, so I thanked him and tried to hang up.

"Anytime, Martha Rae," he replied. "Maybe you should hire me. I'm good at gathering the scuttlebutt around town."

"Not today."

As I sat in my office, I wondered why Carolyn hadn't mentioned Frank's argument with Malcolm. I was going to call her and ask, but decided to stop by the farm instead. Maybe I could help her get the corn maze ready for visitors tonight. After flipping the switch to shut down the station's transmitter, I swung by Ralph's Diner, where I picked up some sandwiches before driving out to Carolyn's.

"What a pleasant surprise," she said after answering her front door.

"What's the latest with Frank?"

"The prosecutor has charged him with Malcolm's murder, but Judge Stone wasn't in town this afternoon, so he couldn't hear Frank's plea. The sheriff is holding him overnight. Said he's afraid Frank might take out his rage on Cyrus McGregor."

"Melvin Pickle is an idiot," I said, shaking my head. "But, what's this I hear about Frank and Malcolm getting into a shouting match last week."

"You must be talking about the zoning board meeting. The McGregors want to sell their farm. Poor Frank. I've never seen him so angry. He's so protective of our farm. It's been in his family for three generations."

"Are you opening the maze tonight?"

"Afraid not," Carolyn said. "The sheriff says it's still a crime scene so we're closed until further notice."

"That's ridiculous," I said. "How can you and Frank keep the farm going if you can't open the maze?"

"I don't know," Carolyn shrugged and broke into tears. I stayed with her for nearly an hour, trying to reassure her that this nightmare would soon be over. Except, I wasn't so sure I believed it myself.

As I turned out of Carolyn's driveway, my plan was to head straight home to my warm, comfy bed. It had been a long day. But, then it struck me. I wonder how Cyrus McGregor has taken the news that Frank murdered his younger brother? Maybe, I should check on him. Besides, a good, outstanding woman like myself should pay her respects to Cyrus in his time of loss.

The McGregor farmhouse is a two-story colonial that was sitting in near darkness as I pulled my Beetle into its circular driveway a few minutes later. The only light emanated from a tiny side window. I walked up to the front door and pounded on it. The McGregors apparently don't believe in doorbells. A minute later, somebody on the other side of the door shouted, "Who's there?"

"It's Martha Rae Folger, Cyrus. I want to ask you a few questions."

Dead silence for a minute. Then, the doorknob rattled and somebody began to open the door. At least to the width of the security chain.

I couldn't see who it was, so I pulled out my cell phone and flipped it open. The phone's screen was bright enough for me to recognize Cyrus McGregor lurking behind his front door. I hadn't seen him in years. Everybody in town calls him a recluse because he rarely ventures about anymore.

"Turn off that darn contraption," he huffed. "What do you want?'"

I flipped my phone shut and tossed it back into my pocketbook. "I'm very sorry about what happened to Malcolm."

"Uh-huh."

"Do you really think Frank shot Malcolm?"

Instead of responding, Cyrus slammed the door in my face. Damn, there I go again. Being too direct. I need to ask more subtle questions. I turned from the doorway and walked back to my car. As I pulled out of the driveway, I spotted a bright red sports car parked beside the side of the house. Wonder which brother owns it? And I here I thought farmers only drove tractors and pickups. Silly me.

♥ ♥ ♥

As I turned to lock my front door on Wednesday morning, I spotted a guy dressed in a long dark trench coat leaning over my Beetle. Tell me he's not soaping my windshield.

"Get away from my car," I shouted.

The person looked up, spotted me running down the sidewalk and took off in the opposite direction. I tried chasing him, but didn't get very far in my heels. But, I did see him climb into a tiny sports car a half block away before he quickly sped off.

I returned to my car and found a typed note under the wiper blade. "Mind your own business, bitch," it read. Now, there's a great way to start the day.

When I arrived at the radio station a short time later, Carolyn was sitting in our tiny newsroom preparing her newscasts.

"What are you doing here?" I asked. "Isn't Frank being arraigned this morning?"

"Not until nine o'clock. I decided to come in and do my newscasts beforehand. Figured it'd help take my mind off things."

I walked over and hugged Carolyn. I was going to tell her about my note, but thought better of it. No sense upsetting her with my news. She had enough news of her own.

Carolyn left for court just before nine. As hour later, she called to say Judge Stone had set Frank's bail at two million dollars. She then asked for the rest of the day off so she could chase down a bail bondsman and meet with a high-priced defense attorney in Indianapolis who'd agreed to take Frank's case.

"We'll lose everything if Frank's convicted," Carolyn cried into the phone.

♥ ♥ ♥

I was well into the second hour of my afternoon talk show when I picked up the line for my next caller.

"Martha Rae, I've found some juicy information about the McGregor rezoning request." Johnny Edwards was on line one.

"Decided against using my private line today?"

Johnny ignored my barb and launched into a fanciful story about how the county's original surveyor must have been dyslectic because a tiny sliver of the McGregor farm rightfully belonged to Frank's family, but the zoning board members agreed to expropriate it under the eminent domain law so the McGregors could obtain a clear deed to their property.

"That may explain why Frank was so upset with Malcolm McGregor, but it doesn't tell us why Cyrus and Malcolm are in such a hurry to sell their farm?"

"I may know the answer to that, too," Johnny said. "An out-of-state meat processor wants to build a plant on their property and he's willing to pay top dollar. The processor has been turned down elsewhere, but a young guy brokering the deal for the McGregors has persuaded two county commissioners to go along with the plan. They're meeting tomorrow night to formally approve the deal."

"That's quite a story, Johnny. What are your sources?"

"Sorry, but a good journalist never reveals his sources," Johnny quipped and abruptly hung up.

Instead of reacting to Johnny's story, my next caller wanted to offer their predictions on Friday night's homecoming football game between the Bartonsville Brigadiers and Morristown Mustangs. After shutting down the station for the night, I jumped in my car and headed for home. I was in the middle of making myself a grilled cheese sandwich when my kitchen phone rang. Who could that be? Maybe, Johnny had an update. He found my private work number yesterday, so why not my unlisted home number, too.

"Is that you, Johnny?" I said after picking up the phone.

Instead, a female voice informed me that she was the triage nurse in the emergency room at Barton County Memorial Hospital.

"We have a Johnny Edwards here," the nurse said. "He's been badly beaten., but he asked us to call you."

"I'll be right there."

It took me ten minutes to drive over to the hospital on the southeastern edge of town. I ran into the emergency room and headed straight for the triage nurse's station.

"I'm here to see Johnny Edwards," I said, slightly out of breath.

"You must be Ms. Folger," the gray-haired nurse behind the counter said. "Mr. Edwards keeps asking for you. Are you related to him?"

"No, I'm his employer." Okay, I lied, but I wanted to see Johnny.

"You can visit him for a minute. He's been heavily sedated, so he's not very coherent."

The nurse escorted me into the large treatment room, pulled back the curtain surrounding Johnny's bed, and reminded me again that I only had a minute.

Johnny appeared to be sleeping as I moved closer to his bed. A gauze bandage covered his head and his face was a mass of cuts and dark bruises. He looked like he'd come out on the losing end of a prize fight.

I leaned down and whispered in his ear. "Johnny, it's me, Martha Rae."

His swollen eyes slowly opened. He tried to turn and face me, but the pain must have been too great.

"What happened to you?"

"I was jumped."

"Where?"

"Leaving the IGA. Guy pulled my wheelchair into the far corner of the parking lot. Tossed me to the ground. Then hit and kicked me several times before taking off."

"Why would anyone do that? Do you have enemies?"

"Not any I don't already know. Never seen the guy before. He was dressed in a dark trench coat. Kept telling me to mind my own business."

Hmmm? Dark trench coat? Mind your own business? Sounded like the guy who'd left that sweetheart message on my car early this morning. I wanted to ask Johnny more questions, but the triage nurse returned. I stepped away from Johnny's bed, but not before telling him that I'd come back tomorrow.

I had trouble sleeping Wednesday night. I couldn't get the image of Johnny out of my mind. And, to think that he ended up in a hospital bed while trying to uncover the real story behind Malcolm McGregor's murder. Johnny must have thought if he solved the mystery, I'd hire him as a reporter. It made me feel guilty.

On Thursday morning, I arrived at the station just after six o'clock. Patty Black was busy previewing some new country songs she'd play on her show, and Carolyn was scurrying about preparing her newscasts. I decided to leave them alone, and went directly to my office where I drew up a list of questions about Malcolm McGregor's murder. When I finished, I went through each one, trying to figure out how I could try to answer them. Johnny must have followed a similar process.

Just past nine, I called Stella Barker, the county recorder of deeds, who confirmed the zoning board had recommended that a tiny sliver of Frank Tinsdale's farm be expropriated in order to build an access road for the proposed meat processing plant. She said a final vote on the plant was taking place at tonight's county commissioners' meeting.

"It's a shame what will happen to Frank's property once that meat processing plant gets built," Stella offered. "Who's going to want to go through their corn maze with those horrid smells coming from next door? And, politicians like to call this economic development."

Stella was right. A meat processing plant probably would mean the end of the Tinsdale's corn maze. And, as much as I hated to admit it, Stella's comment seemed like a powerful motivator for Frank to want to see Malcolm dead in order to save his farm.

Just before noon, I gave Carolyn an update on what I'd found and offered to accompany her to tonight's commissioners meeting. She accepted, and then asked if she could leave early to visit Frank at the county jail. She was still trying to raise the money to post his bail. We agreed to meet back at the station around six thirty.

I was sitting at my desk reviewing this month's advertising sales report when I heard someone walking down the tiled hallway that leads from the back door. It was Carolyn.

"Look what showed up in my mailbox today," she said.

I grabbed the piece of paper out of her hand and quickly read it.

"That changes everything," I shouted.

Commissioner Norman Coyne promptly called the commissioners' meeting to order at seven o'clock. After dispensing with some routine agenda items, he looked out at the largely empty gallery and asked who was prepared to discuss the rezoning of the McGregor farm for commercial/industrial use. The young man sitting next to Cyrus McGregor stood up and approached the podium in front of the commissioners. He launched into a detailed explanation of the proposed meat processing plant. After a few perfunctory questions from the commissioners, the young man sat back down.

"Does anyone else wish to speak before we vote on this matter?" Norman asked.

I raised my hand and stood. "I do."

"What's your interest in this, Martha Rae?"

"I'm speaking for Frank and Carolyn Tinsdale, who oppose the rezoning request."

"Okay, then," Norman said, signaling me to approach the podium. "You can speak on their behalf, but don't take all night."

I launched into an impassioned plea on why building a meat processing plant would be a huge mistake. Even though it might bring some much-needed jobs to the county, I argued that it would ruin the Tinsdale's annual Halloween corn maze. And, wasn't it more important to protect existing property owners' rights than those of out-of-state interests. I was pretty persuasive if I do say so myself.

"Is that it?" Norman asked when I paused to take a breath.

"No, I have something else to show you."

With that, I opened the folder I'd carried with me to the podium. Inside it were photocopies of the note Carolyn had shown me at the radio station. I handed a copy to each of the three commissioners.

"What's this?" Norman demanded.

"It's a letter that Malcolm McGregor wrote to Frank Tinsdale. It showed up in the mail earlier today."

"I object," shouted the young man sitting next to Cyrus McGregor. "What's that have to do with anything?"

"Sit down, sir. I'll give you a chance to speak once we figure out what this is all about. Okay, Martha Rae, go ahead, but make it quick."

"Gladly," I replied. "As you can see from reading the note, Malcolm tells Frank that he's having second thoughts about selling his farm. I also draw your attention to the highlighted line where Malcolm says his friendship with Frank and Carolyn is more important to him than a meat processing plant."

"That's a lie," a voice behind me shouted.

I turned and spotted Cyrus McGregor waving his fists in the air.

"Sit down, Cyrus, and shut up," Norman said. "Martha Rae, this is all very interesting, but how do we know when this letter was written, or even if it's Malcolm's handwriting."

"Good question," I replied. "Here's the envelope the note came in. It's postmarked Monday, the day before Malcolm's body was found in Frank's maze. Carolyn is prepared to say it's Malcolm's handwriting, or perhaps Cyrus would like to confirm that for us."

There was a sudden commotion behind me. I turned to see Cyrus jumping out of his chair and heading toward me. "I'm going to ring your neck, Martha Rae."

"Somebody restrain that man," I heard Norman shout and pound his gavel to gain order. "Under the circumstances, this matter is now tabled. And, this meeting is adjourned."

After shutting down the radio station on Friday night, I dropped by Barton County Memorial Hospital. Johnny Edwards was sitting up in bed, enjoying a bowl of red Jell-O when I entered his room.

"How are you feeling?" I asked.

"Better," he replied. "I heard your show this afternoon."

"Then you heard what happened at last night's commissioner's meeting. Who would have guessed that Cyrus murdered his own brother with Frank's shotgun in order to sell their farm? I hear Cyrus made a full confession to Sheriff Pickle after he was taken into custody. Told the sheriff he was tired of farming, and, wanted to spend the rest of his days lying on the warm beaches in south Florida.

"Did Cyrus act alone?"

"No, his nephew, Eric, helped him. He was the guy who left the nasty note on my car the other morning and I suspect he's the one who beat you up behind the IGA."

"Wait until I get out of here. I'll take care of him."

"Don't worry about Eric. He and Cyrus will be locked up for some time, and it won't be in south Florida."

"What about the Tindale's?"

"They're fine," I said. "Frank was finally released from jail earlier today. He and Carolyn are planning to re-open their corn maze tonight."

"That's terrific," Johnny said, a tiny smile forming on his bruised face. "They're such a nice couple. I have fond memories of running through their maze when I was a kid."

"Listen, Johnny, I need to go so you can get some rest, but there's something else I need to tell you."

"What's that?"

"Drop by the station when you get out of here. I have a job waiting for you."

Originally published in the A Whodunit Halloween *anthology, Pill Hill Press, 2010.*

Harvey's House of Horrors

"Let's do something special for Halloween this year," I suggested to my best friend, Mandy Malone, as we talked on the phone two nights ago.

"What do you have in mind, Candi?" Mandy asked. "Wait, before you answer that question, I'm not passing out candy at my front door this year so don't try to persuade me. The kids in my neighborhood already think I'm a cranky old woman and I want to keep it that way."

"We shouldn't let others think of us as old ladies," I replied. "Yeah, we're in our mid-forties, but we're not ready for the nursing home yet. Remember all the fun we had in our twenties?"

"I remember it all too well," Mandy said. "So, how do you propose we reclaim our youth?"

"Harvey's House of Horrors."

"I thought it closed years ago after Harvey Marcum moved on to that big spooky place below ground."

"It did, but his son, Harvey Junior, reopened it a few days ago and according to one of my clients, it's better than ever. She couldn't stop talking about it today as I did her nails."

Mandy didn't say anything for so long I wondered if she was still there.

"I suppose we could check it out," she finally replied. "I remember Harvey's being a scary place. But you'll need to drive. I don't want some jerk keying my beautiful Jaguar convertible in Harvey's parking lot."

It was just after seven on Halloween night when I pulled into Mandy's semi-circular driveway in my Ford F-150 and laid on the horn. A minute later, Mandy ran out of her McMansion and climbed into my truck.

"Why do you blast your horn every time you pick me up?" she asked. "My neighbors are probably peeking through their blinds and wondering if I've suddenly become a NASCAR fan. And if I run into one of them next week, they'll probably accuse me of lowering property values."

"Sorry, I'll bring my limo the next time. Hey, you didn't say you were dressing retro for our visit to Harvey's."

"It was a last-minute decision," Mandy said. "I was rummaging through my walk-in closet last night when I ran across my old black motorcycle club jacket."

"And it still fits."

"Yeah, it was Butch's wedding gift to me. He was so proud of it. It has the official 'Indy Bad Boys' emblem embroidered on the back and 'Butch's Babe' stenciled in pink italics underneath."

"That's so sentimental. Wearing your first husband's wedding gift. What about Marvin? Did he buy you clothes, too?"

"No, Marvin bought me expensive jewelry and a five-bedroom house before he died," Mandy said. "Look who's talking? Aren't you wearing your ex-husband's high school football jersey?"

"Yeah, I couldn't decide on what to wear, then I spotted Bobby's jersey sitting on a pile of clean clothes I hadn't put away. Normally, I wear it as a nightshirt."

"Won't he want it back if we run into him tonight?"

"Probably, but I'll tell him it was part of our divorce decree, along with this truck he had to turn over to me. He won't know any better."

Harvey's House of Horrors sits just off a narrow gravel road, about a mile south of the Bartonsville town limits. Legend had it that a lumber baron built the now dilapidated three-story structure as a wedding gift for his wife. Once it was completed, his wife refused to live in it. The house was too ostentatious. The man became so upset he chopped up his bride into tiny pieces and buried her remains in the backyard. After the man went to prison, the house stood vacant for several years until Harvey Marcum bought it at a sheriff's auction.

"This place looks like it hasn't changed in twenty years," Mandy said as I steered my truck into Harvey's gravel parking lot.

"You're right, but at least they've added some lights in the lot. Now, we won't fall into a pothole and sprain an ankle."

The young woman at the front door charged us each fifteen dollars. As she handed Mandy back her change, she asked, "Are you a member of the Indy Bad Boys motorcycle club?"

"I was once Butch Muldoon's babe," Mandy said proudly.

"That's so bitchin," the ticket taker replied.

Our tour of the haunted house was a huge disappointment. Like other haunted places, Harvey's had plastic skulls dangling from the ceiling, fake blood spatter on the walls and loud, creepy music playing in the background.

"The decorations look like the same ones Harvey used twenty years ago," Mandy said when we finished the tour. "There was a good inch of dust on everything."

I laughed. "My favorite part was the dude holding up the hatchet in the middle of his forehead after it came unglued. But the guy lying on the floor with the hunting knife sticking out of his chest and the pool of blood around him seemed real."

"This place sucks big time," Mandy said. "So much for reclaiming our youth."

Johnny Edwards was sitting at a table at Ralph's Diner enjoying his breakfast when I walked in Saturday morning. Johnny is a disabled Afghanistan war veteran who gets around town in a motorized wheelchair. He's also a reporter at

WYMN-AM, the town's radio station, and he and I have been known to stick our noses into recent murders in town.

"What's up?" I asked after sitting down next to him.

"Hear about the murder last night?"

"What murder? Where?"

"Harvey's House of Horrors?"

"You're kidding," I said. "Me and Mandy went there last night trying to reclaim our youth."

"See anything out of the ordinary?"

"No, except maybe this one guy. He was lying on the floor with a hunting knife sticking out of his chest."

"Hmmm?" Johnny said before backing away from the table.

"Where are you going?" I asked.

"Sheriff Melvin Pickle is holding a press conference in a half hour. I'm hoping he'll identify the victim and provide some more details about the murder."

"Let me know what he says."

Saturdays at Tips & Toes were often unpredictable. Some-times, we were swamped, especially if a bunch of bridesmaids showed up early and wanted their nails painted the same color. More often, only a handful of regulars had appointments and the day would drag by.

Today, me and Trudy Castle, the salon's other manicurist, had only a few clients, but each one was anxious to tell us of the murder last night at Harvey's House of Horrors and who did it.

"A Satan worshipper probably did it," one of my regulars said confidently.

"Wouldn't a Satan worshipper be more inclined to like the haunted house and not kill anyone who worked there?"

"Oh…I guess maybe you're right, Candi."

Another regular, Rosie Simmons, said she felt sorry for the Marcum sisters after losing their half-brother, Harvey Marcum, Jr., last night.

"How do you know them?" I asked.

"They're renting the house next door to me," Rosie said. "The police were at their place half the night."

"What do you know about them?" I asked.

"Not much," Rosie said. "They've only lived there a few months. But the older one, Martha, seems a little odd."

"In what way?"

"She carries around a hunting knife attached to her belt. How many women do that?"

"None that I know of," I replied.

It was a little after five when Johnny Edwards stepped inside the salon. I was busy working on my last client of the day.

"What's the latest on the murder?" I asked him as I continued painting my customer's nails.

"You're busy," Johnny replied. "Let me grab something to eat at Ralph's and I'll meet you outside when the salon closes at six. Then, we can talk about it."

Johnny was true to his word. He was patiently sitting in his wheelchair when I walked out of work.

"What's going on?" I asked.

"Plenty," Johnny said. "Sheriff Pickle identified the victim as Harvey Marcum, Junior but he refused to divulge any more details about the murder."

"Did he mention if Junior was murdered with a hunting knife?"

"No, he was tight-lipped about the weapon that was used, but I've been busy chasing down leads on my own all day."

"What have you found out?"

"Old Harvey had two daughters when he lived with his first wife in Indianapolis. That was before he divorced her, moved to Bartonsville, married Hilda Jackson, and they had Harvey Junior. Apparently, the half-sisters learned of Junior's plans to re-open the House of Horrors and they wanted in on the action. The sisters felt entitled to any profits from the house's reopening."

"Who told you all that?"

"Believe it or not, your ex-husband. I ran into him earlier today."

"Bobby? How's he involved? Is he dating one of the sisters?"

"I don't know about that," Johnny said. "Bobby did some construction work at Harvey's before it reopened. He said

Junior was always arguing with his half-sisters on how to run the place."

"That's not unusual. Growing up, I fought with my half-brother, Randy, all the time. I don't understand why Sheriff Pickle didn't reveal the weapon used to kill Junior."

"Maybe he's not ready to tip his hand yet to the prime suspect."

"Maybe so, but one of my regulars told me today how Junior's older half-sister always carries a hunting knife on her belt."

"Are you thinking what I'm thinking?" Johnny asked.

"Yeah, we need to check out the sisters."

Johnny insisted on driving to Harvey's House of Horrors. It was easier for him than climbing inside my jacked-up F-150. I didn't complain. His tricked-out van had all the latest gadgets, including hand gears and seat warmers.

"Think the house is still considered a crime scene and it won't be open?" I asked.

"After what Bobby told me today about the half-sisters, my money is on the place being open."

After parking his van in Harvey's parking lot, Johnny and I approached the house's front door.

"How much money did we bet?" Johnny asked after we noticed a bunch of yellow crime tape lying on the ground next to the front entrance.

"Hey, weren't you here last night with that biker chick?" the ticket taker asked me. "If you've come back looking for a refund, you're out of luck. We don't give them."

"No, my friend and I want to speak to the Marcum sisters. Are they around?"

"I'm Stephanie Marcum. My older sister, Martha, is inside. She likes to scare our visitors."

"You don't look very busy tonight?" Johnny said.

"I know," Stephanie replied. "I thought Junior's death might attract more customers. Aren't people curious to see where his murder took place?"

Johnny and I glanced briefly at each other before I told Stephanie I needed to go inside and speak to Martha.

"Sure, but it'll cost you fifteen dollars," she replied. "We're not running a charity here. Sorry, mister, we aren't handicap accessible, so you'll have to wait outside."

Before entering the house, I instructed Johnny to call the cops if I wasn't back in ten minutes.

The first part of the tour was the same as last night. It wasn't until I was halfway through the place when a woman dressed like a zombie jumped out in front of me and shouted, "Want to die?" She waved a large sword in the air.

I let out a loud scream before turning and in a calmer voice asking her, "Are you Martha Marcum?"

"Lady, I'm in costume," she replied, lowering her sword. "You don't ask someone their name when they're in costume."

"Sorry, but I'm just trying to find out more about your half-brother's murder," I said.

Martha had a bewildered look on her face. "In that case, step around the corner so we can talk without anyone hearing us."

I did as Martha asked, including following her into a tiny room off the hallway. Once there, she turned and asked, "Who are you? And, why are you so interested in Junior's murder?"

"I'm Candi DeCarlo," I said, trying to choke back some fake tears. "Harvey and I once dated in high school. He was such a terrific guy. I should have married him back then when I had the chance."

"That's very interesting," Martha said after I finished my story. "Junior spent most of his teen years in reform school. He never went to high school in Bartonsville."

"Oops, my mistake," I said. "I swear that's where I met him. So, can I ask you another question? Why aren't you wearing your hunting knife tonight? I hear you never leave home without it."

"Who told you that?" Martha asked, her voice rising a few octaves.

"I can't reveal my source," I replied. "It's the code of ethics we manicurists now follow with clients. Hairdressers have the same code. What's said in the salon stays in the salon."

"Lady, you're pissing me off," Martha replied, waving her sword in the air. I took that as my cue to rush past Martha and step into the dark hallway again.

Martha followed me out of the room, but a family of five was standing in the hallway. Martha was forced back into character. "Want to die?" I heard her yelling at the family.

I continued down the hallway before ducking into a room that might have been the house's kitchen in a former life. I found a tiny broom closet off to the side and hid inside it. I then pulled out my cell phone and called Johnny. He didn't answer.

What's up with that?

Time to call Mary Donovan, the night dispatcher at the Bartonsville Police Department and one of my regular clients.

"Bartonsville Police Department. What's your emergency?"

"Mary, it's me, Candi. I need your help!"

"What have you done now? Found us another murder victim?"

"No, I'm stuck inside a broom closet at Harvey's House of Horrors. There's a woman chasing after me with a large sword. Hold on a sec. Yeah, I can still hear Martha Marcum dragging her sword along the dark hallway."

"A sword, huh?"

"Yeah, Mary, it's ginormous. I think Martha wants to slice me up into tiny pieces. She suspects I know that she killed her half-brother, Harvey Marcum Junior."

"That's quite a story, Candi," Mary said. "Are you trying to solve another murder on your own?"

"Maybe."

"I could send some officers out there, but the House of Horrors is outside the town limits. You'll have to call the sheriff's department."

"I don't have their number in my contacts list. Besides, Martha is likely to find me any second," I said. "Can you call the sheriff's office for me?"

"Relax, Candi, Johnny Edwards called me a few minutes ago. He told me what's happening out there. I've alerted sheriff's deputies. They should be there momentarily."

I remained scrunched inside the broom closet at least another ten minutes before a Barton County sheriff's deputy wandered into the kitchen and yelled out my name. Once I came out of the closet, the deputy said that he and his fellow officers had taken Martha and Stephanie Marcum into custody for further questioning.

"Your friend, Johnny Edwards, is waiting for you out front," the deputy added.

I thanked him for rescuing me before running outside as fast as I could.

"Johnny, I'm so happy to see you," I said, leaning down and giving him a huge hug.

"Me, too," he replied. "One of the deputies I know said Martha was holding a machete in her hand and it looked like she wanted to use it on you."

"Sword. But, yeah, she's a truly scary person," I said. "I asked her what happened to her hunting knife. She wasn't wearing it tonight."

"I wouldn't have confronted her that way, but I'm glad you're okay," Johnny said. "But, listen, maybe we should stop trying to solve murders on our own for a while. What do you say?"

"Sounds like a good idea to me."

Originally published in Trick or Treats: Tales of All Hallows' Eve, A Speed City Crime Anthology, 2021.

Away in the Manger

"Did you read about baby Jesus this morning?" I asked Joanie Sullivan. She was standing behind the lunch counter at Ralph's Diner brewing a fresh pot of coffee.

"No, I've been too busy," Joanie replied. "What happened to baby Jesus?"

"Somebody stole him," I said, putting down a copy of the Barton County Beacon on the lunch counter. "Right out of his manger at the First United Methodist Church."

"That's horrible," Joanie said as she grabbed the fresh carafe of coffee and headed to the folks sitting at tables in the diner.

"You're darn right, Joanie," I said to myself. "And, maybe I'll do something about it."

♥ ♥ ♥

Tips and Toes was a madhouse on Tuesday. With Christmas less than a week away, every woman in Bartonsville had shown up to have her nails done before she attended a holiday party or Christmas Eve services.

Everyone mentioned baby Jesus as I applied brightly colored holiday polish to their nails and toes. Even our owner, Madge Parsons, seemed visibly upset when she stopped by my nail station to take my lunch order. Earlier, she'd told me and Trudy Castle, the other manicurist in our salon, that we'd have to eat lunch at our stations today, so we could finish our clients' nails without delay.

I was worn out when I left work at six but managed to gather enough strength to drive over to Walmart and then the First United Methodist Church on West Washington Street. I walked around the side of the church where I thought the members met for coffee and donuts after Sunday services. I wasn't sure if anyone was there, but when I tried the doorknob, it opened in my hand.

As I walked down a narrow hallway with offices on either side, I shouted: "Is anyone here?" A moment later, a tall, elderly man with shiny silver hair stepped out of an office and introduced himself as the Reverend Donald Perkins.

"Hi, I'm Candi DeCarlo. I read about someone stealing baby Jesus and I wanted to help. After work, I bought this baby doll at Walmart. It doesn't look much like a boy doll, but I figured he'd be okay in the manger."

I handed the doll box to Rev. Perkins. He examined it closely. "That was very thoughtful of you, Ms. DeCarlo," he finally said. "Are you a churchgoer?"

"Afraid not," I replied. "Sunday is my only day to sleep in, but when I was younger, my mom would drop me and my younger, half-brother, Randy, off at Sunday school if she wasn't too tired after a late night on the town with one of her boyfriends."

"I see," Rev. Perkins said. "Well, I'll tell you what, Ms. DeCarlo. I'm busy writing my Christmas sermon. Why don't you to put this baby Jesus in the manger?"

"Can I?"

I woke up early Wednesday morning still full of Christmas spirit for having bought a new baby Jesus last night. I quickly showered, dressed and stopped by Ralph's Diner.

"The usual, Candi?" Joanie asked as I sat down on a stool at the lunch counter.

"No, today, I'd like two eggs over easy, three strips of crispy bacon and some whole wheat toast," I said.

"What's made you so hungry this morning?" Joanie asked.

"Baby Jesus."

"Huh?"

I quickly told Joanie how I'd bought a doll yesterday after work to replace the baby Jesus stolen from the manger at the Methodist Church.

"That was so nice of you, Candi. Santa's likely to leave you some cool presents under your tree this year."

We weren't as busy at the salon on Wednesday. Madge even let me take a lunch break at Ralph's where I had a grilled cheese sandwich and a medium Diet Dr. Pepper.

It was just after four when Lonnie Sparks, my favorite eighty-year-old client, sat down at my nail station. "What can I do for you today?" I asked

"Paint some red and green ribbons on my nails," Lonnie said. "My older sister from Indianapolis will be visiting me on Christmas Eve. She'll no doubt have some fancy design on her nails, and I can't let her show me up."

As I worked on Lonnie's nails, we talked about what was happening around town. When I mentioned how baby Jesus was back in his manger, Lonnie interrupted me.

"What are you talking about? The manger was empty as I drove by the church on my way to the salon."

After work, I drove by the Methodist Church. Lonnie was right. No baby Jesus. I checked my wallet to see if I had enough cash before heading to Walmart. Christmas tips come in handy this time of year.

There weren't too many dolls left in the toy aisle at Walmart, and none that could pass for baby Jesus. I found a store clerk and asked if he had any more dolls out back.

"Sorry, lady," the clerk replied. "What you see is what we've got left. However, there are some new Barbie dolls on display at the cash registers if you'd like one of them."

Barbie as baby Jesus? I don't think so.

I finally settled on a life-sized doll with shoulder-length blond hair. She'd have to do. After climbing into my truck in the parking lot, I opened the glove compartment and grabbed my portable manicure kit. I carry it everywhere. I took the scissors in the kit and cut off the doll's hair.

Once I finished, I drove back to the Methodist Church. I thought of telling Rev. Perkins about my second baby Jesus, but I figured he was still busy with his sermon.

I placed the doll in the manger before jumping into my F-150 to head home for dinner. As I was pulling away from the curb, I noticed someone slowly walking down the sidewalk in front of the church. The person stopped next to the nativity scene.

I couldn't believe what happened next. The person leaned down and picked up baby Jesus and began walking away. I sat in stunned silence in my truck. I couldn't believe what was happening. I grabbed my cell phone to call the Bartonsville Police Department, but then thought better of it. By the time the cops arrived, the baby Jesus thief would be long gone. So, I decided to wait a few minutes and follow the thief myself.

The baby Jesus snatcher turned left at the corner and continued walking slowly along Jefferson Street before stopping in front of a gigantic two-story Victorian house. The thief then climbed a set of front steps before stepping inside the house.

I turned off my truck's ignition. Should I call the cops now that I know where the baby Jesus thief lives? Something about this whole situation didn't seem right. Why would someone who lives in a magnificent-looking house want to steal baby Jesus? I decided to find out on my own.

I marched up the front steps and rang the doorbell. A minute went by before a tiny, white-haired woman in a bright red dress opened the front door.

"Can I help you?" she asked in a soft voice.

"Yes, you can. My name is Candi DeCarlo. I just saw someone steal baby Jesus from his manger on Washington Street and enter this house."

"Oh, my, I'm afraid you've caught me red-handed," the woman said, sticking her arms out in front of me. "Are you going to handcuff me?"

"I'm not a cop, but I'd like to talk to you."

"Of course, how rude of me. Making you stand out there in the cold. Please come inside. My name is Emma Lou Pettijohn, but everyone calls me Lou."

I followed Lou inside. She hung my rabbit-fur jacket on a wooden coat rack in the large foyer before showing me into her living room. Once there, Lou told me to make myself at home in one of the straight-back chairs. She would be right back.

Several large wooden cabinets filled the living room. Each contained shelves of gorgeous antique porcelain dolls in elaborate knitted dresses. And, on the window seat below the room's large picture window sat three dolls. Two dressed in knitted sleepers. The one minus its blond hair was still naked.

"I hope you like hot chocolate," Lou said upon her return. She was carrying two mugs in her hands. She set one down on the table next to my chair.

"I noticed you admiring the baby Jesus dolls," Lou said as she sat in a chair next to me.

"Yes," I replied. "I see you've already dressed two of them."

"Oh, yes dear," Lou replied. "The Farmer's Almanac predicts a blustery winter this year. If the dolls aren't wearing proper clothing, I'm afraid they may catch pneumonia. And we wouldn't want that now, would we?"

I didn't know what to say so I picked up my mug of hot chocolate and took a sip. It was stone cold. Lou must have run the hot chocolate mix under her water tap instead of boiling some water.

"Is your drink okay?" she asked.

"Yes," I replied. I couldn't tell this sweet little lady the truth. "It's fine. I don't like it too hot."

"Me, too," Lou said. "If it's too hot, you could scald your tongue."

"You have a lovely doll collection," I said, changing the subject. "Did you make all the outfits?"

"Yes, dear. My husband didn't want children, so these dolls became my children. In the beginning, Marcus would only let me have a few dolls, but after he passed away, I used some of his money to buy more and the cabinets, too. I also have dolls in an upstairs bedroom. Probably a hundred in all."

"Wow, that's quite a collection," I said. "You must be very proud of each one. Now, can we talk about baby Jesus?"

"Of course."

"I'm sure you know he was born in a manger because Joseph and Mary couldn't find any room at the inns in Bethlehem."

"Yes, I know that story very well."

"Then, you also know that Joseph and Mary didn't have much money so they could only clothe Jesus in a blanket and not a fancy knitted outfit. I have no idea why the Methodists want to keep baby Jesus naked, because he really should be wrapped in a blanket. That way, the nativity scene will be historically accurate."

"I think I understand what you're saying, young lady," Lou said. "Instead of a knitted outfit, baby Jesus should wear a baby blanket. I have several upstairs."

"Great. Wrap up baby Jesus in one of them and take him back to the manger tomorrow."

"I'll do it."

Mary Donovan, a dispatcher with the Bartonsville Police Department, was on time for her appointment Thursday afternoon. As I applied some ruby red polish to her nails, I asked her if she'd ever heard of Emma Lou Pettijohn.

"The squirrel lady who lives in that big Victorian on Jefferson Street?"

"Squirrel lady?"

"Sorry, some of our officers call her by that name."

"Why?"

"Each fall she calls us, worried about the squirrels living in her backyard. She's convinced her neighbor's dog chases them into the street where they are run over. She gets upset because they don't get to finish gathering nuts and berries to feed their families over the winter. Why are you asking about her?"

"I ran into her last night," I said.

"What was she doing?"

"Stealing baby Jesus."

"Did she tell you why she did it?" Mary asked.

"Yeah, she was afraid he'd catch pneumonia if he wasn't dressed in a warm knitted outfit."

"I'm not surprised?" Mary said. "The woman is a little looney."

"Not looney. Just a little lonely. Does she have any family to help care for her?"

"She has a niece who lives in Chicago, but she has a family of her own and doesn't visit too often. Want me to send someone around to her place and have her return baby Jesus?"

"No, I already persuaded her to wrap him in a blanket and return him to the manger."

"Candi, you should be a social worker instead of a manicurist."

After Mandy Malone's third husband passed away, my best friend since kindergarten and I began a new Christmas Eve tradition. We'd eat dinner at a fancy restaurant in Indianapolis and then drive home to Mandy's place where we'd split a bottle of champagne and complain about why there weren't any decent men to date in Bartonsville.

This year, Mandy won a week-long Caribbean cruise for two after winning a company sales promotion at her discount tire stores. She wanted to take me, but she figured Madge wouldn't let me go because it's the salon's busiest time of the year. So Mandy took her daughter-in-law instead.

I was going to ask Madge out to dinner on Christmas Eve, but she left early to meet her girlfriends at a riverboat casino along the Ohio River. Madge also let Trudy leave early so she could cook a special Christmas Eve dinner for her husband.

I ended up closing Tips and Toes on my own. It was then that I thought of Emma Lou Pettijohn. She was probably sitting all alone in that big house of hers. I called her to see if she'd join me for dinner at the Chinese restaurant next to Walmart. I knew it would be open late on Christmas Eve.

Lou loved our Schezwan dinner for two but insisted on using chopsticks instead of a fork. As a result, dinner took longer than normal. She couldn't get her fried rice to stay on the chopsticks.

"What do you want to do now?" Lou asked me after our bill and fortune cookies arrived. I glanced at my Betty Boop watch. It was just after eleven o'clock.

"Let's attend midnight services at the Methodist Church," I said. "We also can check on baby Jesus."

"That's a wonderful idea," Lou said. "But, I'm afraid I haven't been inside a church in a long time."

"Me either."

Ten minutes later, I managed to find a parking space near the front of the church. As Lou and I exited my truck and walked towards the nativity scene, I could see that she'd returned baby Jesus like I'd asked her. He was covered in a red, white and blue blanket.

"What do you think of him, Candi?" she asked.

"He looks very patriotic lying there."

The Mysterious Mincemeat Murder

"Where should we eat dinner on Christmas Eve?" my best friend, Mandy Malone, asked after I picked up my phone.

"You didn't win another Caribbean cruise?" I asked.

"Nope, my stores finished third in this year's Goodyear winter tire sales promotion. No cruise for me. Just a form letter from the company's president."

Too bad. I was hoping to go with you this year.

"So, what's it going to be? Steak or seafood?"

"Let's do something different this year," I said.

"Like what?"

"Martha Rae Folger told me about an opportunity the other day when she stopped by the salon."

"What?" Mandy asked.

"The administrator at the new assisted-living facility is giving her staff the night off on Christmas Eve, so they can spend time with their families before they return to work on

Christmas Day. She's inviting local folks to treat her residents to a potluck dinner on Christmas Eve and a musical program."

"Wait a minute," Mandy said. "You want me to spend Christmas Eve spoon feeding some toothless old woman instead of eating dinner at an upscale restaurant in Indianapolis. No way."

"Mandy, don't be such a Scrooge," I said. "It'll be fun. Helping the less fortunate is what Christmas is all about. Besides, we shouldn't be filling our faces with food that isn't on our diets. And, we'll get to sing Christmas carols to the residents. I love to sing."

"The only singing I do is in my shower."

"Martha Rae plans to interview the volunteers on her radio show all week."

"She does?" Mandy asked.

"Yeah, and whoever donates the turkey and ham for the dinner will be mentioned several times on her show."

"Maybe volunteering at the Springs isn't such a bad idea," Mandy said. "After all, if Martha Rae is behind it, everyone in town will know about it, right?"

"Right," I said. "So, you're willing to help?"

"Why not. People need to know my business supports the less fortunate."

"Great. There's just one more thing," I said. "I want Emma Lou Pettijohn to join us."

"Who?"

"Emma Lou," I said. "Remember, she's the older woman I ate Christmas Eve dinner with last year when you were on your cruise."

"Is she the one who kept stealing the naked baby Jesus from the manger at First United Methodist Church because she thought he'd catch pneumonia?"

"Yes. I've already talked to her about that. She's promised to leave him alone this year if the church ladies wrap him in a warm blanket."

It was nearing six o'clock when Mandy and I picked up Emma Lou in front of her gigantic, two-story Victorian house on East Washington Street and drove her to the Springs of Bartonsville. Margaret Sullivan, the facility's administrator, greeted us at the main entrance.

"Good evening, ladies," she said with a big smile. "What have you brought us?"

"A pre-cooked turkey breast and a spiral ham," Mandy said, pointing to the heavy bags in my arms. "You'll need to warm them in an oven for a few minutes."

"And, what did you bring?" Ms. Sullivan said, turning to Emma Lou.

"A tray of mincemeat tarts," she proudly replied. "I made them myself, using my mother's old English recipe."

"How interesting," Ms. Sullivan said. "I've never eaten one before. Let's put them on the dessert table in the dining room."

As we followed behind Ms. Sullivan and Emma Lou, I turned to Mandy and whispered, "What a beautiful place. I'd love to live here when I get older."

"Save the tips from your manicures, and who knows," Mandy replied. "Someday, this could be all yours."

The potluck dinner went off without too many problems. For a bunch of frail-looking old people, the residents had some hearty appetites with many requesting seconds. It was as if they hadn't eaten in a week.

Mandy spent her time asking folks how they enjoyed the turkey and ham that she bought for the dinner. It was like she'd been transported back in time to when she would schmooze her diners as the hostess at the Barton County Country Club.

Martha Rae remained in the kitchen, helping Ms. Sullivan prepare bowls of vegetables and mashed potatoes and slicing the meat.

I ran between the kitchen and dining room delivering platters of meat and bowls of food to each table. Emma Lou followed behind me like a little puppy dog.

"Is everyone finished with their dinners?" Martha Rae asked after I'd returned to the kitchen for what seemed like the umpteenth time.

"I sure hope so," I said. "My feet are killing me. I haven't been a waitress for a few years. I'm out of shape."

Just then, we heard loud shrieks coming from the dining room. We ran out of the kitchen and noticed a white-haired gentleman dressed in a tweed jacket, white shirt and wearing an ugly-looking Christmas tie lying on the floor. He had been sitting at a table full of women and apparently had fallen out of his chair. I knelt beside him and felt for a pulse.

"He's dead," I said as I stood up a few seconds later.

"What?" Ms. Sullivan shouted. "That's impossible! Mr. Worthington can't be dead. He's one of my healthiest residents."

The ladies at the table suddenly began screeching all at once. It took a few minutes for me to quiet them down.

"Mandy, call the cops and let them know what's happened," I said. "Ms. Sullivan, send your residents back to their apartments except the ones sitting with Mr. Worthington."

"What should I do?" Martha Rae asked.

"You're a radio host," I replied. "Take Emma Lou and these ladies to the far corner of the dining room and ask them what made Mr. Worthington keel over."

"The cops are on their way," Mandy said as we watched Martha Rae and the ladies walk away. "Think the old guy had a heart attack or a stroke?"

"I don't know," I replied. "But if he was as healthy as Ms. Sullivan said, something's definitely not right here."

Nate Sloan and Frank Turner of the Bartonsville Police Department arrived at the assisted-living facility within five minutes of Mandy's call.

"What are you two doing here?" Nate asked when he spotted us.

"We served the residents dinner until this guy on the floor keeled over and died," I said.

"Who is he?" Frank asked.

"All I know is that his name is Geoffrey Worthington and he was eating dinner with a bunch of ladies," I replied. "Where's Chief Cobb?"

"Dan drove to Indianapolis for the holidays, but we'll call and get him back here right away," Nate said. "I'll also call the coroner."

"Where are the women who were sitting with this guy?" Frank asked.

"Talking to Martha Rae," I said, pointing to the far corner of the dining room.

"Oh, great, that's all we need is her nosing around in the middle of everything," Frank replied. "It's liable to end up on her radio show."

Frank and Nate walked over to Martha Rae, said something briefly to her and Emma Lou, before they began interviewing the women themselves.

"What did Nate and Frank say?" I asked when Martha Rae and Emma Lou returned to where we were standing.

"They told us to mind our own business and stay out of their investigation," Martha Rae said.

"And, those nasty women said Geoffrey died after eating one of my mincemeat tarts," Emma Lou said.

It took me, Mandy and Martha Rae at least a half hour to calm down Emma Lou and persuade her that her mincemeat tarts couldn't possibly have killed Mr. Worthington even though someone kept yelling that the tarts were poisoned. The breakthrough came when I agreed to eat one of them myself.

I know. What was I thinking?

"Are you crazy?" Mandy said as she followed me to the dessert table. "You could drop dead just like that old guy. Who knows what your friend put in her tarts?"

"Listen, I trust that she followed her Mom's recipe," I said, placing a tart on a small plate and returning to the dinner table. Once there, I took a tiny bite of the tart. The pastry was very flaky. The ingredients thick and fruity.

"What's in this tart?" I asked Emma Lou, taking a second bite.

"Raisins, currants, lemon zest, shredded suet, chopped mixed peel, brown sugar and a touch of nutmeg," she replied.

"Is that all?"

"My mother's recipe calls for brandy, but the jar of mincemeat I bought at the store was non-alcoholic, so I added my own alcohol."

"Wait a minute," Mandy said. "That tart is laced with alcohol? Let me taste it."

"But, a minute ago you were afraid for me to try it," I said. "What changed your mind?"

"It contains alcohol?" Mandy said, grabbing the tart out of my hand and taking a big bite.

"Emma Lou, this is delicious," Mandy said. "I need a tart of my own." She stood up and headed for the dessert table.

As I looked up, I noticed Dr. William Armstrong enter the dining room. He's been a general practice physician in Bartonsville and the county's coroner for a hundred years. My mom took me to him when I was a kid.

Nate and Frank spoke briefly to him before steering the doctor to the dead guy. I waited a few minutes before I wandered over to where Dr. Armstrong was examining the body.

"What did he die of?" I asked.

"Who are you?""

"Candi DeCarlo," I replied. "I was a patient of yours when I was a kid. And, I'm the one who checked his pulse after he fell over."

"That was very brave of you, Ms. DeCarlo," Dr. Armstrong said. "Most people won't go anywhere near a dead person. I won't know what caused his death until I get him back to the morgue and can perform a more thorough exam."

"Well?" Mandy asked when I returned to the table.

"Doc doesn't know what caused Mr. Worthington's death," I said. "Maybe he was allergic to an ingredient in the tart. Like kids who get sick from eating peanut butter. Or, maybe he was allergic to the brandy."

"That's a horrible thought," Mandy said.

Dr. Armstrong spent another half hour examining Mr. Worthington before he released his body to the paramedics. After they had all left, Nate and Frank approached our table.

"Got anything more to say about what happened tonight?" Nate asked.

"No," I replied. "We were in the kitchen when Mr. Worthington keeled over. We didn't see anything."

"Are you done interviewing the residents?" Martha Rae asked.

"For now," Frank said. "We'll return tomorrow if Dr. Armstrong's autopsy raises any new questions. Chief Cobb also should be back in town by then."

As Nate and Frank left, Margaret Sullivan walked up to our table.

"Get your residents calmed down?" I asked.

"I hope so," Ms. Sullivan replied. "I'm actually more concerned about their children once word gets out about Mr. Worthington's death. They'll want to move their parents to a safer facility."

"Sorry to hear that," I said. "So, what should we do now?"

"Let's help Margaret clean the kitchen, so her staff doesn't have a mess when they return to work tomorrow," Martha Rae said.

"Excellent idea," Mandy said, biting into another mincemeat tart. "Candi and Emma Lou can straighten the dining room while the rest of us work in the kitchen."

♥ ♥ ♥

"Did you know any of the women sitting with Mr. Worthington?" I asked Emma Lou as we wiped down the tables in the dining room.

"Mildred McDonald," Emma Lou replied. "Our husbands were once business partners. The four of us would get together regularly to play bridge, but after our husbands passed away, Mildred and I drifted apart."

"What was her theory about Mr. Worthington dying?" I asked.

"She thinks it was my mincemeat tart," Emma Lou replied. "He either choked on it or it poisoned him."

"She said that to your face?" I said. "I thought you'd been friends for years."

"Her comment really wasn't aimed at me," Emma Lou said. "It was more a statement of disappointment."

"What do you mean?"

"Geoffrey Worthington was considered a prized catch."

"Huh?"

"Not many men live here," Emma Lou said. "Geoffrey was a recent widower. He was handsome and appeared to be in good health. My guess is several women had their eyes on him."

"They wanted to marry him?"

"No, silly, just looking for a roll in the hay."

"Oh," I said, my face suddenly turning red. "Think Mildred killed Mr. Worthington?"

"Doubt it, she loved her husband, Edgar, too much," Emma Lou said. "Besides, he left her a fortune. Mildred wouldn't be interested in squandering it on another man."

"Did she have any other suspects in mind besides you?"

"If she did, Mildred wasn't about to say anything in front of the others," Emma Lou said. "These women wouldn't let a man – even a dead one – get in the way of their friendships."

"Maybe we should talk to her privately," I said. "Since Mandy and I didn't die after eating your tarts, I doubt Mr. Worthington was poisoned, but who knows. Nate and Frank didn't seem to have any clue about what happened to him or have a suspect in mind. Maybe, we can figure it out on our own."

"That sounds wonderful," Emma Lou said. "I've always wanted to be a detective like the ones on TV."

We walked to the facility's main entrance where Emma Lou and I found Mildred McDonald's mailbox and the number of her apartment. It took us only a few minutes to locate her place. We gently knocked on her door.

A minute went by before a short, white-haired woman in an attractive-looking pink satin housecoat opened her door.

"What are you doing here, Emma Lou?" Mildred McDonald asked.

"My friend, Candi, and I want to ask you a few questions about tonight," Emma Lou said. "Can we come in?"

"I guess so, but I don't what more I can tell you," Mildred said, opening her door wider to let us inside. Her apartment was gorgeous. She'd obviously spent part of Edgar's money buying some expensive furniture. It put my apartment to shame. Emma Lou and I sat on a large floral-patterned sofa in the living room. Mildred sat across from us in a straight-back chair.

"Emma Lou says you think Mr. Worthington either choked to death on one of her mincemeat tarts, or he was poisoned," I said. "Is that correct?"

"That's what I said," Mildred replied.

"Sorry, but I don't think he choked to death," I said. "When I knelt beside him to check his pulse, his mouth was clear. No sign of the tart stuck in his mouth or throat. Ms. Sullivan says he was her healthiest resident, so while a heart attack is certainly possible, I'm guessing that didn't cause his death. That leaves poisoning."

"Why do you think he was poisoned, Mildred?" Emma Lou asked. "Know something you're not telling us?"

"Of course not," Mildred said. "I don't know. It just popped into my head. I was watching a *Law and Order* rerun before dinner. A woman was accused of poisoning her husband for his insurance money. The episode must have stuck with me."

Emma Lou turned to me and rolled her eyes.

"Mildred, what do you remember right before Mr. Worthington collapsed on the floor?" I asked.

"Geoffrey was finishing the last bite of his dinner when I jumped up and headed to the dessert table. He was a very proper Englishman, so I figured he knew all about mincemeat tarts and would enjoy one for dessert. Betty Foster and Vivian Appleton apparently had the same idea. Suddenly the three of us were each grabbing a tart and a small plate and rushing back to the table.

"Whose tart did Geoffrey eat?" Emma Lou asked.

"I don't know," Mildred replied. "I slipped on the carpet underneath the dessert table on my way back. By the time I got to the dinner table, Geoffrey had bitten into a tart. I don't know if it was Betty's or Vivian's."

"What can you tell us about Betty and Vivian?" I asked.

"They're gold diggers," Mildred said with a straight face. "A single man doesn't stand a chance around that pair. They're all over the poor guy until they find out he either isn't rich or can't perform where it counts."

"What was Mr. Worthington's situation?" Emma Lou asked.

"Everyone figured he was wealthy, but Geoffrey hadn't been here long enough for anyone to know if he was a player," Mildred said.

"A player?" I asked.

"Yeah, you know, a guy who enjoys women fussing over him."

"Sounds like we should chat with Betty and Vivian," Emma Lou said.

"I agree."

Emma Lou and I thanked Mildred for her time and headed to the apartments of the two gold diggers. Mildred had given us their numbers.

"Still think Mr. Worthington was poisoned?" Emma Lou asked.

"I don't know," I replied. "But I'm guessing if he was allergic to an ingredient in your tarts, he wouldn't have eaten it. He would know. After all, he was an Englishman, right?"

"Right."

Betty Foster's apartment was three doors down from Mildred's place. We knocked several times, but there was no response.

"Suppose she's already asleep?" I asked.

"Doubt it," Emma Lou responded. "If she's like most old women, she can't sleep at night and likely stays up watching TV or reading a book."

I glanced at my Betty Boop watch.

"It's approaching nine o'clock," I said. "Maybe we should check on Vivian."

Her place was on the other side of the facility. It took us ten minutes to walk there. A huge Christmas wreath covered her door, making it hard to find a clear space to knock.

A minute went by before a tall woman with rust-colored hair opened her door and asked what we wanted.

"We want to ask you about Mr. Worthington," I said. "Can we come in?"

Vivian invited us into her living room. Another woman was already sitting in a chair.

"This is my friend, Betty Foster," Vivian said. "Who are you two?"

"I'm Candi and this is Emma Lou," I said. "We helped serve you dinner tonight."

"I thought you looked familiar," Betty said. "What can we do for you?"

"You were sitting with Geoffrey Worthington and each offered him a mincemeat tart for dessert, is that right?" I said.

"So?" Vivian said.

"What do you think happened to Geoffrey?" Emma Lou said. I could tell she was still smarting from Mildred's comment about her tart poisoning him.

"Poor Geoffrey wasn't poisoned like Mildred thinks," Vivian said. "She has an overactive imagination. She watches too many cop shows on TV."

"What about you, Betty?" I asked.

She shrugged and didn't say anything.

Emma Lou and I continued questioning Betty and Vivian, but they didn't have any more insights into Mr. Worthington's death. I wondered if they were hiding something. Emma Lou and I were about to leave when I asked Vivian if I could use her bathroom.

"It's at the end of the hall," she said.

After relieving myself, I washed my hands and looked in the mirror above her sink. I looked awful. Trudy Castle and I worked on clients until nearly five o'clock. Our boss, Madge Parsons, doesn't believe in closing Tips & Toes early, even on Christmas Eve.

I was about to turn and leave when I was suddenly overcome by a desire to peek inside Vivian's medicine cabinet.

The devil made me do it.

Amid several bottles of perfume, mascara, and tubes of lipstick was a small dark bottle. I picked it up.

"Sodium cyanide?" I said aloud as I read the label. "What's Vivian doing with it?"

I didn't wait to answer my own question. I needed to get back to the living room before everyone wondered why I was lingering in the bathroom.

"Is everything okay?" Vivian asked as I sat down on her couch next to Emma Lou.

"Fine," I said, trying not to look too guilty.

Emma Lou and I stayed a few more minutes before we excused ourselves and left Vivian's apartment.

"Find anything interesting in Vivian's bathroom?" Emma Lou asked as we walked back to the facility's dining room.

"Why'd you say that?" I asked.

"Vivian and Betty were wondering what was taking you so long in there," Emma Lou said.

"I found a bottle of sodium cyanide in Vivian's medicine cabinet," I said. "She might have used it to poison Geoffrey."

It was another five minutes before Emma Lou and I returned to the dining room. Mandy, Martha Rae and Margaret Sullivan were sitting at a table each enjoying a cup of coffee.

"Where have you two been?" Mandy asked. "We were worried about you."

"Candi and I did a little detective work of our own," Emma Lou said.

"What?" Martha Rae said.

I told them how after meeting Emma Lou's old friend, Mildred McDonald, we ended up visiting Betty Foster and Vivian Appleton.

"Not those two," Margaret said when I finished.

"Why'd you say that?"

"They're the two residents who cause me the most grief."

"How so?" I asked.

"They're constantly competing to see which one can attract the most men in this place," Margaret said. "They both viewed Geoffrey as a huge prize."

"Who was winning?" Mandy asked

"Neither, I'm afraid," Margaret said. "Geoffrey was still in mourning over his wife's death and wasn't interested in a female companion, and especially not Betty or Vivian."

"What makes you so sure?" Martha Rae asked.

"He came to my office last week. Asked me to speak to them. He wanted to be left alone. I spoke to Betty and Vivian two days ago."

"Maybe they were still angry at your meeting," I said. "But, was that enough to want to see Mr. Worthington dead?"

"Hard to say," Margaret replied, taking another sip of her coffee. "They're very competitive and they don't like to take `no' for an answer."

"Can I ask another question?" I said. "What did Vivian's husband do for a living?"

"Her last one was a pharmacist," Margaret said. "Owned his own independent pharmacy before he passed away."

I stood up and started to walk away.

"Where are you going now?" Mandy said.

"I'm calling the cops," I said. "I know who poisoned Geoffrey Worthington."

"What's going on?" Nate Sloan and Frank Turner asked after entering the Springs of Bartonsville dining room a half hour later.

"Candi knows who poisoned Geoffrey Worthington," Emma Lou said.

"She does, does she?" Frank said. "Interfering in police business again, Candi? Hasn't Chief Cobb already warned you to mind your business when it comes to police matters?"

"Yes," I said. "But, I'm pretty sure I've got the right person this time."

"Let's hear it then," Nate said.

I quickly explained how Emma Lou and I visited Betty Foster and Vivian Appleton and how I accidently found a bottle of sodium cyanide in Vivian's medicine cabinet.

"So, now you're now convinced this Vivian woman poisoned Worthington," Frank asked.

"Yup."

"What makes you so sure, Candi?" Nate asked.

"Margaret says her husband was a pharmacist before he passed away."

"What do you think, Frank?" Nate said. "Should we check out Candi's story?"

"Why not," Frank said. "We've got nothing better to do tonight. It beats riding around town in a squad car with a busted heater."

Emma Lou and I gave Nate and Frank directions to Vivian's apartment.

"You should all go home and leave the police work to us," Frank said as he and Nate walked away.

"Should we leave like they said?" Mandy asked.

"No," the rest of us shouted.

It was another hour before Nate and Frank returned to the dining room with Betty Foster and Vivian Appleton in tow.

"Was I right about the murderer?" I asked proudly.

"No," Frank replied. "You had the wrong person."

"What?"

"As we questioned them about Mr. Worthington's death, Ms. Foster broke down and confessed to poisoning him," Nate said. "She was afraid he liked Vivian more. And, if she couldn't have him, Betty didn't want Vivian to win his heart."

"She stole the bottle of sodium cyanide out of my medicine cabinet," Vivian said. "Here I thought we were best friends. And, she put it back tonight before you showed up at my apartment. Now that I think about it, you must have peeked in my cabinet, too."

Vivian looked directly at me, but I began admiring her house slippers and didn't say anything.

"What's going to happen now?" Martha Rae asked.

"We're taking Ms. Foster into custody tonight. We will meet with Chief Cobb and the coroner in the morning to decide if Mr. Worthington was in fact poisoned before we charge her with anything," Frank said.

"Make sure Chief Cobb knows I helped solve your case," I said.

"I'm sure he'll want to issue you a citizen's commendation once he finds out," Frank said as he grabbed Betty Foster's arm and headed for the main entrance.

"What should we do now?" Emma Lou asked after they left.

"I don't know about the rest of you, but I'm going home," Martha Rae said. "I'm beat."

"Us, too," said Margaret Sullivan and Vivian Appleton.

"What about us?" Mandy asked.

"I've got an idea," Emma Lou said.

"What?" I asked.

"Let's attend midnight services at First United Methodist Church," Emma Lou said. "I was so busy making mincemeat tarts the past few days that I didn't check on baby Jesus."

"Speaking of mincemeat tarts," Mandy said as we left the assisted-living facility. "Are there any left?"

Originally published in Homicide for the Holidays Anthology, *Blue River Press, 2018.*

Acknowledgements

First, I'd like to thank members of the Speed City Chapter of Sisters in Crime who edited the anthologies where my short stories first appeared. They include, in alphabetical order: Diana Catt, Marianne Halbert, Tony Perona, Brenda K. Stewart and Wanda Lou Willis.

Jean M. Goldstrom also deserves my admiration for publishing a couple of my stories at Whortleberry Press and Jessy Marie Roberts for doing the same at Pill Hill Press.

Finally, members of my critique group, *In Mysterious Company*, deserve a ton of credit for their always helpful advice on the stories they reviewed for this anthology.

Also, special thanks to Candice Cooper for designing the cover and Robin Surface of Fideli Publishing for all her hard work in seeing this anthology through the production process.

If you enjoyed Candi's cozy exploits, be sure to check out Hangnails

When Bartonsville bank president, Walter Morgan, fails to keep his weekly hangnail treatment, Candi DeCarlo, a manicurist at the Tips & Toes salon, goes looking for him. She finds him – her biggest tipper – slumped over his desk with a large hunting knife sticking out of his back.

It doesn't help that the town's hunky new Police Chief, Dan Cobb, initially considers Candi a person of interest.

However, when Sylvia Wilson is arrested the next day, Candi swings into action. She can't believe her daughter's former second-grade teacher and the head of the town's Youth Center is the murderer.

Candi joins forces with disabled Army veteran, Johnny Edwards, to find the real killer. But they didn't anticipate receiving threatening notes or being kidnapped at gunpoint.

Available now at Amazon.com, Barnes & Noble and other online retailers everywhere.